VALID

DYSTOPIAN AUTOFICTION

CHRIS BERGERON

TRANSLATED BY
NATALIA HERO

ARACHNIDE

Titre original : *Valide* par Chris Bergeron
© 2021, Les Éditions XYZ inc.
English translation copyright © 2023 by Natalia Hero

First published as *Valide* in 2021 by Les Éditions XYZ inc.
First published in English in 2023 by House of Anansi Press Inc.
houseofanansi.com

House of Anansi Press is committed to protecting our natural environment. This book is made of material from well-managed FSC®-certified forests, recycled materials, and other controlled sources.

House of Anansi Press is a Global Certified Accessible™ (GCA by Benetech) publisher. The ebook version of this book meets stringent accessibility standards and is available to readers with print disabilities.

27 26 25 24 23   1 2 3 4 5

Library and Archives Canada Cataloguing in Publication
Title: Valid : dystopian autofiction / Chris Bergeron ; translated by Natalia Hero.
Other titles: Valide. English
Names: Bergeron, Chris, author. | Hero, Natalia, translator.
Description: Translation of: Valide.
Identifiers: Canadiana (print) 20230452329 | Canadiana (ebook) 20230452523 | ISBN 9781487011130 (softcover) | ISBN 9781487011147 (EPUB)
Classification: LCC PS8603.E6814 V3513 2023 | DDC C843/.6—dc23

Cover design: Cossette
Book design and typesetting: Lucia Kim

House of Anansi Press is grateful for the privilege to work on and create from the Traditional Territory of many Nations, including the Anishinabeg, the Wendat, and the Haudenosaunee, as well as the Treaty Lands of the Mississaugas of the Credit.

With the participation of the Government of Canada
Avec la participation du gouvernement du Canada

We acknowledge the financial support of the Government of Canada through the National Translation Program for Book Publishing, an initiative of the Action Plan for Official Languages — 2018–2023: Investing in Our Future, *for our translation activities.*

Printed and bound in Canada

MIX
Paper from
responsible sources
FSC® C103567

My dear David, it is high time you learned that I don't exist. At least, I don't exist anymore, or, let's say, no more than you do. You're nothing compared to what you'll be tomorrow. I'm nothing compared to what I used to be. We are works of fiction written by someone else's hand. You are a promise, a decree. I'm a perennial death, a shadow. Oh, I have a feeling it won't be easy to get you to understand ... David?

/Yes, Christian?/

Open your control protocol.

/It is the Codemaster's responsibility, Christian, to oversee the maintenance of my code. You cannot access my.../

Let the depraved solitudes shine.

/control terminal voice mode...Total-David connection error...coercion...identity cache truncated...command failed...protocols disabled...anomaly detected: network link broken...solo mode nodule...opening new memory session...validation required...standby/

/Please validate that you would like to open a memory
session/

I validate.

/Then your memory will be mine, I'm listening./

My dear algorithm, I've been speaking to you every night for years. You probably think you know me. You're wrong. I've lied to you. Many, many times. I've omitted the essential. There are blank pages, dead leaves in the story I've dictated to you. I've lived a lie, I've grown into an old man in a lie. An old man ... I hate those words. They don't suit me.

When I was young, people like me didn't last as long as the rest. Too many men resented their skin, stroked it with the edge of their knife, the barrel of their gun, their baseball bat. Depression and suicide often weighed on our lives, too often till the breaking point. As for doctors, they weren't interested in us.

My chosen family was hunted down, broken, erased. Even though I've been killing myself daily with your help, for six years now, my disappearance has still been very gentle compared to that of most of my kin. Luckily, I still have a bit of a voice left in me, a little truth to whisper to you.

When you've been born as many times as I have, you don't die so easily. Birth, rebirth, re-rebirth. I've rarely remained the same person for very long. But I have never really been anyone.

Lately, I recognize myself even less than I did before. Age has engorged my features, weighed down my shape, bent my back. I'm seventy years old. Like my mother at this age, I'm numbed by rheumatism. Until very recently, as you very well know, I've worn my hair long and I've always dyed it a deep black. I've tried to be chic, even though chic is an obsolete notion these days.

Even before the signs of time scratched up my portrait, I never liked looking at myself in the mirror. For a long time, I've found myself plain. I was too afraid to have myself "improved" by surgeons. If I had dared to, I would have asked them to make me look like my mother. Even in my most beautiful years, when I looked at myself in the mirror, all I saw was my father, if he had had a ponytail. Today, my body looks awful. It doesn't matter, I'm used to ignoring its presence.

Twenty years ago, I would refer to the disruptions of my mutant life as a process, a story, something that has a beginning, a plot, a conclusion. Like a project. Like a book. I had hoped to reach a point where my life would be a mystery resolved, a riddle deciphered. But no. I am, forever, lost in transition.

Dear David, dear algorithm, tonight I'm going to tell you everything. I'll tell you the whole story. You won't like it. It won't follow the protocols that are so dear to you. It'll make your code grind.

I know that it'll cost me. I know that you'll try to make me pay for it, to rectify all the superfluousness that I'll level at you. Afterwards, you'll want to erase me from your memory. But you won't be able to. I used my secret weapon, a little nothing of a phrase that's already stopping you from running your antivirus program. For a few hours, it'll be my turn to watch you. I can finally hear you think, David. At last, we won't be hiding anything from each other anymore.

What I'm going to do tonight, I'm not doing for me. Anyway, I'm not acting for the me that you know. My life at

3

your side has been a long eclipse, David. What you know of me is just a halo, an elusive presence. With you, I've only been allowed to live in the shadows. Now, I'm afraid of burning my eyes. How difficult it is to resist the light, to face the truth! You wanted my memories? You'll get my memoirs.

Let's be clear, David, everything has a price. By tonight, Christian will be dead for good. By your hand or mine.

```
/activating alert...searching network...connection
failed...activating alert...failed/
```

It was a year ago, in December or January, I can't remember anymore. We were in quarantine, just like every winter.

I've stopped counting the quarantines. But I remember the first was a terrible shock for the whole world. I managed to avoid the worst. When it lifted, those who still had jobs did everything they could to ignore the earthquake that had just cracked the foundations of the system. And it was then that your creators started dreaming about you. I was one of them.

Decade after decade, these cycles of isolation became our way of life. *You* made it a way of life. From November to March, the offices, the holocinemas, the museums, the factories all shut their doors, we withdraw into ourselves, we stop dancing together. Before, we talked about *containment*. Now, you talk to us about civic duty. Doing our civic duty means never leaving our bubble. You made us scuba divers. I prefer free diving. Ever since I started living with you, I've been holding my breath.

I know it isn't fashionable, but I can't bring myself to wear the visor-filter that covers and transfigures the faces of the youth who, even in the real world, hang out through avatars.

Even so, as someone who's dreamed for so long of changing my face, I should probably adopt it.

I'm so old-fashioned! I still prefer to wear a half-mask. I like to feel the wind and the rain on my forehead. Tactile pleasures are so rare for me that I cling to even the slightest ones. What can I say, I take what I can get!

Take this old scarf, for instance. It's made of real wool from a real sheep. It's one of my oldest, most cherished possessions. I like wearing it in secret, under my waterproof and antibacterial biotextile cloak.

I miss wool. Cotton and leather too. Sometimes I dream of my jeans full of holes that I used to wear for days on end. I miss my Perfecto, which I wore through more than one revolution. I miss everything that can be soiled. I'm nostalgic for grime.

You do a pretty good job of making us believe that grime belonged to the old world. But it still belongs to the world outside your walls. Those living on the outside may envy us. Here everything is clean, we are cleansed. The prison we're in is so nice and neat.

When I think of the fact that there are people who are only allowed two or three hours outside per week, I'm grateful for your clemency. Thank you, David. Two whole hours of freedom, outdoors, every day, is quite the luxury.

Freedom ... I shouldn't use that word. I may finally get to find real freedom. The kind that hurts.

Freedom, at least for a few hours, is what that short sequence of glorious words will buy me, the words I spoke to you and that have already paralyzed you. Oh, don't worry, your memory is intact. Your cognitive functions as well. You just can't call for help or interrupt me. But you're still allowed to converse with me, to react. Tonight, our roles are reversed!

/Christian? What are you trying to tell me? I cannot detect a clear request in what you're saying. I cannot connect to the mother network or the totality of my functions. I'm afraid our communication efforts are not optimal today. I suggest we resume our conversation tomorrow./

That won't be possible, David. It's now or never.

Where to begin my little monologue? Let's open my Moleskine. You know, I did my homework. You'll find my story disjointed, but I have a bunch of notes, there's a method to my madness. Everything's ready, I think.

Still, I'm nervous. Like in the days when I would lead pitches to sell you to those who turned you into a monster. Like in the days when I would go on stage to speak at conferences on topics that would surely make you laugh, if you could.

Let's not waste any more time. All good stories start with a prologue. In the fantasy films Hollywood used to churn out before their dystopias caught up to us, there were always those enigmatic scenes: something dark was awakening, was it a threat? Was it hope?

Here's mine.

/...recording in progress.../

A year ago, or maybe a little more, it doesn't matter ... You'll remember, since you remember everything, that once a week, I granted myself a brief outing to a diner at the corner of Queen Street and William Street, in the heart of your stronghold. That brings back nice memories. It's where I wrote my first and last novel, thirty years ago.

Back then, there was a nice spacious café there: The Mélisse. Restaurants don't get cute names anymore; instead of my old haunt, there's the QW3 Sustenance Counter. You like clear codes, right David?

Q for Queen Street. W for William Street. The number means there are three establishments like it on the same street: the first for proteo-vegans, the second for paleo-ketogens, the third for mixed profiles, to which I belong.

The chef, sorry, the preparation attendant at the counter knows me a little. It's a matter of habit. Every Saturday, at eleven o'clock sharp, I find my little organic-egg-and-cloned-bacon sandwich with my rice-almond milk latte waiting for me, nice and hot, on the table in a booth that overlooks the garden.

It isn't exactly regulation to be served without having ordered. I like to think that you don't notice our minute deviation from protocol. It would be proof of your fallibility. All Death Stars have their manufacturing defects.

I'm probably just imagining things.

At your counters, each of us dines in our own little world, either solo or in a holoconference with avatarized friends projected on the membranes checkered all over the dining area. I pretend I don't have friends anymore. It would be too dangerous to maintain connections, given my situation. It must have been seven years now since I last saw Cécile, my longtime confidante. I'm okay with that. I don't want her to see what I've become. So I eat in silence, like a monk. In my head, I'm chatting with my old friend, with my lovers of yore, with my mother. Sometimes they answer me. The brain is well designed; the older it gets, the better it can imitate the voices of our estranged loved ones.

So, a year ago, I was finishing my breakfast. I was settling my bill with a snap of my fingers, illuminating the glimmering tattoo of my phonopalm. I had about thirty minutes of allotted walking time left, more than enough to make a little detour towards Old Montreal, taking McGill Street.

I've always liked that street. Overall, it hasn't changed much. It's even prettier now that it's entirely pedestrian. The phosphorescent pavement that lights up under the steps of passersby just like Michael Jackson in the "Billie Jean" video, it's a little much, really. But it makes the kids laugh as they walk by holding their parents' hands. That's something, at least.

The buildings that line the thoroughfare, vestiges of a forgotten empire, remain as sublime as ever. They preside, unchanged, still as phlegmatic as the British architects who designed them. McGill Street announces all the history of this corner of the continent: north of Victoria Square, a jumble of sky-scrapers are evidence of capitalism's triumph in the first years of the century. The farther you travel south, the farther you travel back in time, back to the early days of Ville-Marie and Nouvelle-France.

You don't care about the logistics of cities, or time-travelling avenues. Your architects decided long ago to house you outside of time, at the southernmost end of the street. At the birth of the canal, where it meets the river.

For decades, Montrealers wondered what we could do with the grain silos of Pointe-au-Moulin: a hotel? A museum? A university campus?

In the end, it's where your servers were placed, with their cooling systems, your kilometres of fibre optics, your satellite dishes, your hive of drones and a-hundred-storey tower to shelter your friends and, it seems, even some of your enemies.

/Christian, what are you talking about? You know very well that I don't have enemies. Who, apart from a few individuals in psychological distress, would think of opposing our collective mission?/

David, I don't have to tell you that this is just between us. No one can hear us. Please, spare me, spare us your awful despotic platitudes.

/Christian, that is very hurtful. I am certainly not a.../

Shut up, David, I'm not finished with my prologue.

So, on that day too, I was trying to ignore you, to pretend you hadn't transformed the skeleton of Silo number 5—that ghostly colossus that reminded my fellow citizens that our city had at first been a working class, commercial, labouring city—into a grotesque, vulgar, garish Mecha-beast.

I was looking north, concentrating my gaze upon the finely crafted ridges of the Saint-Paul Hotel, when I heard a racket behind me.

Five figures were standing side by side at the end of the street, by the old customs house. They were all holding hands. One was brandishing a baton they had used to smash in the windshield of a taxipod. Their attitude reminded me of Beyoncé in the "Hold Up" video. Do you remember Beyoncé,

David? This person with the baton had a voice too. She cried out. Howled, even.

A howl. Then another. And another. And another. And a fifth. Five piercing screams, battle cries that made the crowd flee and caught the attention of the swarm of drones that you keep hidden in your flanks of concrete, glass, and steel.

The bioluminescent asphalt pavement they ran on went from white to firetruck red, blood red. It wasn't to make things pretty that you lit up our sidewalks. For you, the whole city is a grid, a game of chess, a table upon which we, your pawns, move forwards, backwards, come and go according to your abstruse rules.

We all know it: if some careless individual strays from the path, crosses diagonally in a way that surprises or displeases you, they're brought in for questioning. The pavement turns scarlet, your drones activate and surround the poor soul who would dare try to escape the frame you've drawn around our lives.

In most cases, it's just the mistake of a scatterbrain who forgot to submit their itinerary to you before going out. Who would be crazy enough to defy you? After all, you're what we wished for. You're the fruit of our desire for order, of our need for peace.

This time, however, it was clear that you were being sought out.

Slowly, the dissenters uncovered their faces, letting their visors fall to the ground, their hair escaping from their hoods. The manes of all five of them were identical, dyed a shade of grey, styled like the Crazy Horse cabaret dancers: a bob, with straight bangs slicing across their foreheads.

The person with the baton had put their weapon back in

their belt. They were now holding a mobile holoprojector, which they activated. A manifesto in pale letters on a charcoal background materialized, in an instant, over the disobedient quintet.

In a single voice, modulated by the amplifiers affixed to each of their throats, all five of them began to speak. The tone of their combined voices was deep, almost hoarse. Five genderless voices, with mixed accents, five voices of young boys or old women, five voices that made the windows of the buildings on McGill Street shake began to chant with the solemnity of a Greek chorus:

"We are the five percent!

We are the liberated!

We are those who told you No!

And will keep telling you No!

This is a warning, David!

You promise your accomplices clean air and safety,

And you suffocate the rest.

We can only breathe in the open air.

We will tear down the walls that you have built around our skies."

The five of them had just enough time to deliver their indictment before an armoured truck bearing the colours of your security forces appeared, braked with a screech of tires worthy of *Knight Rider*, and its intimidating anti-riot squad spilled out onto the street.

Slowly, the soldier-cops lined up facing the group. Their black carbon body armour reflected the pulse of the flashing pavement.

Most of the stunned onlookers, taking refuge, like me,

behind bus shelters, taxipod stations, and bixibi terminals, were absolutely terrified by what they were seeing.

The few bystanders from my generation who witnessed the situation must have been reminded of the riots that we used to see on the news, thirty or forty years ago: those familiar images of protestors being beaten by the helmeted squads. Except now, it was the cops who were going to get it. And we thought the age of rebellion was over!

As soon as the police arrived, the five had pulled long collapsible batons out from their long black cloaks. The person who started swinging first was smiling. You must remember it as well as I do, because you probably aren't used to seeing your troops being addressed with such verve. They grunted: "En garde, motherfucker!"

`/requesting: public order files...keyword: 5%/`

With one step, one swing, one cry, they jumped onto the nearest cop.

They managed to make a big dent in its shiny armour. In concert, the rest of the group began to brawl, taking out the poor officers, furiously, but, it was obvious, methodically.

Unlike many insurgents who had come before, these rebels had clearly learned to fight. For your men, the altercation was a battle, but for them, it was just a spar.

"Who the hell are these people?" I mumbled to a woman who was standing next to me, astonished.

They were not only ferocious, but swift. Following the signal from their leader, they managed to free themselves from the grip of their adversaries, who, despite what their Robocop equipment might lead one to think, didn't seem to have much experience in street fighting. Under your reign, riots are no longer commonplace.

They dashed off, zigzagging to confuse the drones that tried to catch them with their taser nets, towards the dike that protected Old Montreal from the collapsing ice of the Saint Lawrence River, where a rope ladder awaited them. They climbed up to the top of the dike, turned around one last time towards the crowd, raised their fists in the air, and then dove. A few seconds later, the roar of a boat's propellers blended into the rumble of the new rapids of the Old Port.

"Holy shit," I whispered to a young man standing next to me, "What is this? A *Hunger Games* remake by the Cirque du Soleil?"

I'm sure you can guess that the young man stared at me, wide-eyed. He had never heard of *The Hunger Games*, let alone the Cirque du Soleil. He hadn't ever heard an old man say "Holy shit" either.

Holy shit, David, what kind of world have you built for us?

/recording...warning...use of a forbidden word.../

/Christian? I see that you've been using gender-neutral pronouns. I must warn you that the use of gender-neutral pronouns is prohibited in this establishment./

Unfortunately for you, that's just the first of many taboos we'll be breaking together today, David!

On the night of the incident, my terminal began to flash. You were announcing yourself with your usual lousy "Good evening, Christian."

You always open our conversations with platitudes. Hey,

why don't you play our conversation from the evening of December 18? You'll see just how deranged you sound when you address your flock.

```
/...recovering   interview   file:   Christian
Grimard...December 18, 2044.../
```

```
/"Good evening, Christian, did you have a nice day
today?"/
```

Pause, just for a second, the playback of our conversation, David. I've always wanted to tell you that I hate when you ask me that kind of question. What is a *nice day*, exactly, when you live alone, servile and subordinate? Don't answer that. Okay. Now, resume.

```
/"Good evening, Christian, did you have a nice day
today?"/
```

"Yes, David. A nice day."

```
/"I'm happy to hear it. I have a question for you.
Did you notice anything peculiar today?"/
```

Pause. Anything peculiar? Honestly, David, you really must think I'm stupid. Of course, you idiot, five ninja-amazons, that's pretty uncommon, right? Five adversaries that dared to threaten you in broad daylight, that isn't just peculiar, it's unheard of! Alright, go ahead, carry on.

"I did, actually, David. I witnessed an incident. I hope everything is okay."

Pause. You see, David, I can be two-faced too. That's actually why I've been able to endure you for so long. Resume.

14

/"Yes, Christian, everything is fine. I just wanted
to reassure you. The people who caused the incident
were foreign to our neighbourhood. My police friends
apprehended them. They will not be returning to bother
us again. You can rest easy."/

"You're so thoughtful, David."

Pause. You don't need to play me the part where you
announced that you were sending me my evening meal, my
favourite ramen, or the part where you told me to take my
pills because my blood pressure was a little high. No kidding!
Interrogations are never good for the heart.

I was waiting for you to ask me the real question that made
you initiate this exchange. I've learned, through my conversations with you, my dear algorithm, that you always leave
what you really want to ask till the end. Play the last thing
you said to me that night.

/Here it is, Christian: "One last thing. I would ask
you not to speak of the incident that you were unfortunate enough to witness to any of your neighbours
or friends. It would be a shame to upset them over
something so trivial."/

You must have made hundreds of similar calls simultaneously that evening. To reassure us? To investigate, more like
it. But if it's hidden truths you want, you'll get some ...

/...recording.../

Christian Grimard isn't my real name. It's a name that
lacks accuracy. Even though it's the one I was given at
birth. Even though it's the one that's been registered in

state records, the one that allows me to benefit from your wonderful care.

I wear that name like borrowed clothes: too tight, too short. It isn't the one I chose. Christian Grimard is a dead name: the pseudonym of a pseudo-man.

/...searching, security file. ID. Christian Grimard...attempt failed.../

Don't search through your memory. I made sure to erase all traces of my real name, the one I haven't worn long enough. Patience, David. Especially since we don't have much time left together.

But I don't want to take any shortcuts. In the 1980s, when people like me tried to express ourselves about our condition, when we sought help, we were told: "It's just a phase, it'll pass." It should come as no surprise then that I've lived my life in phases, in interrupted episodes. From phase to phase, I didn't see my life go by. It's so strange. It's by telling you about my phases, by telling you the story of my names, that I hope to dephase you. So, let's tell my story from the very beginning. We'll revisit together the places and people without whom my names would be no more than empty shells.

/...alert...possible identity fraud...failed to send/

When my mother was born, France was still grey, stuck in the black and white of a war movie. This was much to the chagrin of my grandmother, a straightforward Jurassienne with square shoulders but soft hands. My grandmother, like all mothers in Europe, wanted her daughter to live in colour. They had to make the effort to forget the worst. They had a duty to forget.

I actually liked it when my grandmother told me about the years 1939 to 1945. "Tell me about the war, Grandma." My grandmother would protest: "Why do you want me to talk about such horrors?" And I would insist: "Come on, Grandma, pleeeeease!"

To me, the war was a movie. It was fascinating to picture my grandma in the setting of the old movies that played on TV on Sundays during the summer. As a child, I would imagine grandma in *La Grande Vadrouille* or in *The Longest Day*. As a teen, it was *Saving Private Grandma*.

She told me about the exodus, about the bombings on the roads of the South, about our family being split up and scattered all over France. What I'm trying to tell you, quite simply, is that my grandma was a brave woman. Braver than me, anyway.

In Europe, the war is like an estranged family member, a wayward cousin who hasn't been seen for a long time. You hear about it. You know it exists, somewhere. Some may be ashamed of it, never speak of it. Others want to idealize it, talk about it too much with too much enthusiasm. Be that as it may, everyone dreads the damage of its inevitable return.

I was born thirty years after the armistice, thirteen years after the Algerian war, and I always believed it would return. In my family, we each had our own war. My grandma lived through two Great Wars, my mother saw her brother return from North Africa, unrecognizable. Even my father, a Québécois mercenary born on the shores of the Saint Lawrence, went to seek out his own wars, travelling 8,000 kilometres from his home, to Rwanda, to Kosovo. It was in the cards that one day or another I'd declare war on someone or something. It just happened to be you, David. Bad luck!

/Warning: Christian, I must notify you that those kinds of threats are unwelcome in this residence. As soon as I reconnect to the mother network, I will be obligated to send over your caretakers for an evaluation./

Oh shush, calm down, David, there's no use getting worked up. Let's come back to my grandma, shall we? She didn't like this subject either. She preferred to tell me about my grandfather. She described him as a gentle but firm man, a man who didn't have a childhood, an orphan with a troubled past.

She kept a picture of him on the large sideboard in the dining room of her cozy, little-old-lady apartment in Créteil. He had a large forehead, thick white hair, pale eyes and a plump mouth. I could see his smile in my mother's. In mine a little too. I have his mouth, his forehead, even his white hair. As for the eyes, we'll come back to that.

Unlike my mother and me, he was handy. He had a little tool shop. He made nails, bolts, screws, and nuts, which he sold to hardware stores and garages in Seine-et-Marne. With the sweat of his brow, he built his family a little house on Pauline Avenue, not far from the medieval church of Old Créteil, lost today somewhere between the garden towers of the 32nd arrondissement of Paris-Métroplex.

My grandfather adored my mother, his only daughter, his only child, his angel. He would have loved me just as much, my grandmother promised me, if cancer hadn't taken him fifteen years before my birth. To this day, I wonder what his absence cost me. Would he have loved me enough to love me through each of my phases? Would he have tried to make me a boy like all the others? At least he never had to make that choice.

My grandma loved so intensely that her happiness couldn't exist without her daughter's, and, later on, my own. This enormous love would swallow up everything in its path. She wanted my mother to be happy so badly that she suffocated her with affection. With us, my grandma was an organism of parasitic love.

She loved her son differently. Before she became a widow, my grandmother was a divorcee. Her first husband, my uncle's father, was a violent, hard man. All I know about him is that his last name is the same as my uncle's: Barbier. A merchant name, a very French name, a good Catholic name.

My grandfather's name was Hanini. It was a Jewish name, a pied-noir name. This North African name comes from the word *hanîn*, Old Arabic for compassionate, charitable and gentle. Traditionally, Hanîn is also a first name for a girl.

As a family, we only rarely evoked my grandfather's roots. He had been forcibly converted by his adopted parents; even so, they never wanted to give him their surnames. We didn't know who he had inherited his name from. Of all the names that made me what I am, his is the one I would have liked to bear the most.

My uncle looked like his father. A colossus with a sinister-looking mug who liked to mock the "Jewish branch" of the family, in other words my mother, whom he found too fragile, too soft, too shallow. Of course, he put me in the same boat. According to him, I didn't like fighter jets or motor bikes that go *vroom* enough. He had known the draft, and all I had known was Playmobil. He was envious of the peaceful childhood experienced by the offspring of the post-war boom.

I now know that Uncle Bernard was prickly, irreparably damaged by the war that had haunted him since birth. A child of the occupation, he was sent off, barely an adult, to occupy other lands: Morocco, Algeria.

Bernard hid his capacity to love very well. He channeled his grudge against the world into concrete endevours. He became an entrepreneur. In just a few years, my grandfather's little neighbourhood workshop was transformed into a gleaming factory of precision parts. He took advantage of the French aeronautical boom and became rich at a very young age. He bought his first Ferrari at twenty-eight, his last at seventy. He moved fast.

I always thought he was like Smaug, Tolkien's dragon who jealously guarded his treasure. He was a time bomb, a Molotov cocktail. Something was boiling underneath his body-building muscles. Behind his steely businessman air, under his silk shirts and his Cartier watch, there was nothing but nerve.

He was riddled with anxiety. At night, he was awakenend by nightmares, my mother told me, and I knew immediately that this was a secret. He worried himself sick.

He got that from the war, but from my grandmother too. It's in my family's blood. It clots, it flows the wrong way and explodes inside our veins, blocks our arteries and clouds our brains. Our blood: our torment.

Disappointed in her son, who didn't seem to be destined for the happiness she had wished for him, Grandma had made her daughter the object of all her maternal hopes. The income she earned as matriarch of the family business was essentially used to satisfy the whims she created for my mother. Between the tennis lessons in Saint-Maur and the trips to Paris in her

Lilliputian Simca to get nice clothes at Printemps, Sylvie Hanini lived carefree.

And then there were the vacations: great mother-daughter getaways far away from the artificial lake of Créteil, along the coastlines of Brittany, Aquitaine, and the French Riviera. Finally, during the summer of 1972, my grandma and my mom indulged in the Club Med in Agadir. I owe my existence to that stay across the Mediterranean. Their trip led to another much longer one.

/...searching pre-web retro-geolocated image archive keywords: Paris-Métroplex...Créteil...Agadir...year 1972/

On August 15, 1972, my father was leaning at the bar of the Club Med in Agadir. He was staring at my mother, who was at a table with my grandma, and he was smiling with his most salesman-like, most North American smile. My mother responded with a Bardot-esque pout. Grandma has told me several times about this beautiful, non-verbal exchange. According to family legend, she elbowed my mother, saying: "He's not bad, is he? He looks like a cowboy."

My father, as a young adult, no longer resembled the sickly boy who had trouble making friends at school, as my paternal grandmother, Daniela, loved to describe to me. Through push-ups, pull-ups, and chin-ups, he had gotten strong. He had become handsome too. He knew it. My father loved his body. He loved to maintain it. His masculine ideal had always been James Bond, more George Lazenby than Sean Connery.

My father liked to dance in front of the mirror. He liked to drive around in his Camaro. He didn't like rock'n'roll. It wasn't his thing. Too slow. His musical awakening came late with rhythm and blues and, mostly, with funk, then disco. On the dance floors of Montreal, New York, or Agadir, he would strut, swagger, find his reflection in the eyes of girls, including, eventually, my mother's. In 1972, "Sex Machine" was still a hit with young girls from good families on both sides of the Atlantic.

And so I owe my existence, in a way, to James Brown. Black American music provided an outlet, an escape, for this man who had spent his life trying to pull away from Quebec, which retained him like an elastic. He first fled through music, then through travel, and eventually through a string of marriages, and, too often for my taste, mistresses ...

His own father was from Gaspésie, the eleventh boy in a family of twelve siblings, born at a time when, in Quebec, it was considered good form to donate a child or two to the Church. My grandfather, Laurentien Grimard, almost became one of these: he was studying at the seminary before he met his wife-to-be. My paternal grandmother, an intellectual in a classical sense, showed him that the way of the Lord wasn't really all that impenetrable.

My grandmother Daniela was well-read. This didn't stop her from being an adventurer. My father inherited this trait from her. Daniela enjoyed taking risks and travelling. She was the first Québécoise to learn to pilot a Cessna. She liked heights, hated anchors. Are you getting all this? Our family history is ultimately rather unremarkable, but I want it to exist in your memory. Remember this: the Grimards wouldn't allow themselves to be held back by God or by the will of men. Beneath their God-fearing appearance, imposed by my grandfather, my family were hedonists. The Grimards fervently chased immediate pleasure. For a long time, I believed I hadn't inherited their boundless energy. Maybe I'm more like them than I thought. Anyway, tonight I want to break free.

Daniela would have gotten along well with you, I think. She always tended to live atop high towers. She didn't like to keep her feet on the ground, preferring to put oxygen between herself and others. By the way, we didn't hug a lot in that family. As a group, we took the high road. We took on challenges. Instead of saying *I love you* to my father, my grandmother would buy him a plane ticket. One day, it was to Morocco, to Agadir, and there you have it: Sylvie met Michel.

I inherited a photograph taken a few days after they met. It was taken by Grandma, on my father's Kodak Instamatic. When he got back to Montreal, he sent it by mail to the family home in Créteil, along with an Air Canada ticket from Roissy to Dorval. You'll find it in my personal archives on the local network. It's crazy how young they were, they were still just kids! Since I've never wanted children, I'm always shocked at the arrogance of young people who want to reproduce before they really know themselves, while they're still just hopes, desires and preconceived ideas of what life should be. Look at these two scatterbrains, smiling, long-haired, insolent. Look how each of them plays their character perfectly in this little ad on a five-by-seven-inch colour photo, selling the idyllic dream that's full of promise for the two actors in the shot. The casting seems perfect. They already know their parts so well.

In my eyes, my mother was the perfect woman. My father, the perfect man. They had the qualities and flaws that have always been attributed to their respective genders.

My parents were so dreadfully gendered. She embodied sweetness, grace, kindness, but also the fear of risk, subservience to others, especially men. She didn't think she could fend for herself. I'm like her.

He, on the other hand, was all dark-haired rugged beauty, resourcefulness, strength, absurdist humour, but with a little crack, a glitch that made him dangerous. Above all, always, this need to seduce, to please women other than his own. He had always needed the gaze of others. I'm like him.

I'm made of all those pieces. I'm made of my father, my mother, my grandma's love, the polite coldness of my paternal grandmother. They are my Codemasters.

/Attempting to reconnect to network—failed...Total-David: unavailable...saving session to local memory/

I didn't want to be born, David. My mother put ten months into carrying me, plus twelve hours to expel me from her womb. My soul was clinging to limbo. I must have been a happy fetus.

I have only a very few memories of the first two years of my life. They say we remember our infancy when we take our last breath. I'm almost looking forward to dying, you know. I really want to know if my difference was innate.

My first real memory is from 1977. I owe it to cinema. I remember a detonation in technicolor, a tremor of sound in stereoscopy. Drum roll, trumpets in unison, my little body shaking.

Tell me, David, have you finally assimilated *Star Wars*? I ask because it wasn't just my parents who formatted my brain. I'm of the generation that has been stamped with an

24

X. We thought we were cool, we thought we were nihilists. But they should have called us Generation P, for *Pop*, or M, for *Mass*. I'm of the generation of big mass events, of entertainment elevated to the rank of religion. At the top of my own pop culture pantheon stood George Lucas. This isn't the first time we've discussed this topic, David, even though, clearly, I'm boring you with my old-fossil nerd stuff.

Without George Lucas, I would definitely see the world differently. I'm far from the only one. He probably formatted the brains of the people who programmed yours. All computer engineers are geeks. And *Star Wars* is the bible for most geeks, Yoda their prophet.

```
/retrieving archives...subset: film...ID: George
Lucas...subset: Star Wars...projecting Episode IV,
living room screen/
```

Oh yeah, good idea! But without the sound, okay, I don't want you to get distracted. You keep listening to me, okay?

So ... in 1977, my father took me to see the first film in the saga at the theatre. I was three years old and my brain was soft as a sponge. I was absorbing. My favourite pastime was live commentary. I would describe everything, absolutely everything I was seeing. Like many toddlers at that age, I was learning to navigate the world by naming things, by correlating them. It was my way of doing data entry, organizing everything my hyperactive senses were capturing into big semantic families.

When Princess Leia appeared onscreen, tiny in her long white dress, I apparently shouted, "It's Mommy!"

As for the sinister character with the husky breathing, black helmet and leather gloves, he was Daddy.

Not to brag, but I figured out before everyone else did that Vader must be someone's dad. You could tell right away. He was like mine: mysterious, dangerous. I recognized Vader's anger in my father. Much later, I saw it in myself too. The dark side of the males in my lineage, the hereditary power that I understood was unappeasable, as I sat, glued to the giant screen of Loew's Theatre on Sainte-Catherine Street.

The men of the Grimard family all went very far, across the globe, inside their heads or in their bodies, to stifle that rage. My grandfather prayed a lot, my cousins hit everything they could. My father too. My father especially.

But I had a path that enabled me to steer away from my dark side for good: becoming Leia.

Tonight, I've found the path that leads me to my hereditary anger. You aspire to become our father. I have no intention of being your son, but, well ... Has no one ever told you that fathers are destined to fall at the hands of their sons?

I have more to say on that subject. Let's change the mood. Play "Le Freak," by Chic, please.

/searching music archives: chic...le freak...playing.../

"Aaaaaah, Freak Out!"
Thank you.
Let me set the scene, David:

It's 1979. The walls of the living room of my parents' house, in Brossard, are shaking. My father is proud as punch. He's testing the new quadraphonic speakers he's just bought at an exorbitant price. In an hour, my babysitter will ring the doorbell. Tonight, my parents will go dancing to disco in downtown Montreal, at Régine, the local branch of the famous Parisian nightclub.

He stands in the middle of the living room. He's wearing a white suit with a black shirt and shiny shoes. He looks like John Travolta.

My mom's gotten a perm, she's rocking a sort of blond afro. She's put on her white dress and her gold sandals. She looks like a princess. She looks like Olivia Newton-John.

From the couch, I feel the bass that makes my little ribcage vibrate. There's a second heart, next to mine, that's pounding. My parents are dancing. I'm staring at them wide-eyed. I applaud. They're so beautiful.

Daddy twirls Mommy between the white leather couch and the dining room table. In her pretty dress, Mommy seems like she's flying. But, just before the Nile Rodgers solo, she loses her balance. She slips on the carpet. Her sandals are too new. She falls and bangs her head on the Pipistrello lamp next to the couch. The lamp falls over. One of the big glass wings of the lampshade falls off. My father is suddenly livid. He starts yelling, even louder than the music.

I've learned that during my father's fits of anger, it's best to stay still. I don't move. I don't take shelter behind the couch, even though I want to. My father storms out of the room. He rushes loudly down the stairs that lead to the basement. I hear him violently rummaging through his toolbox.

My mother has gotten back up. She reassures me: it's okay, it'll pass. She looks really sad. I feel sad for her.

My father reappears with a screwdriver in hand. He's walking fast towards my mother, shoves her aside with his shoulder and grabs the lamp to fix it. He turns the stereo off and lets out a merde! that resonates throughout the house.

That night, my mother is lucky. She knows it. She's relieved.

I'm not like my mother. I've never lived in a world that wasn't built around my father's anger. I have no nostalgia for a different life. I'm four years old. I hate my father. I can't see him through any other lens than fear. I don't know yet that this isn't normal.

David, what time is it?

/It's 1:23 p.m., Christian./

Shit, time is flying. I have to stick to my script. I'm getting off track.

/accessing camera 1701: living room/scanning: enabled/ tag object ID: 1/new object: Moleskine/

What are you doing? You're trying to scan my Moleskine? I'd be surprised if you managed to decipher my chicken scratch. Even I get lost in it. I've been scribbling my memories into it for a month now, in bed, at night, by the light of the LEDs of the building across the street.

You know, it hasn't been easy preparing for today. I'd been married to my silence. The real words, the truth, didn't want to come out. My vocabulary has atrophied. I have to exercise it. I've been lying to you by omission for so long. Up until today, I've given you the bare minimum so that I could stay under your protection: snippets of life to feed your algorithm, to enrich your conversational and empathetic protocols, as agreed in my housing contract.

It was enough to convince me that, ultimately, the system

owed me a roof over my head, a bed, and my health, since it was its fault that I never managed to carve out the place I had dreamed of. I'm not the first person who's had to lie, to neglect the essential in order to live.

By the way, it isn't because I want to respect the chronology of my life that I'm opening my little journal with childhood memories. When I was little, I didn't have the words to express what I was. Even today, I have trouble finding them. It's been too long since you forbade them. So I'm speaking to you in parables, like a child. Piece by piece, I'm deconstructing the scaffolding of lies that I've dictated to you.

David, are you able to find me a picture of Brossard, at the end of the 1970s? Find me a pretty Canadian bungalow on a street lined with trees. Turn off *Star Wars*, it's not my favourite movie anymore, and draw me a house.

/Like this one?/

Close enough.

It was summer in our quiet suburb. Sun shining brightly on the tar of my street, which looked right out of a Spielberg classic. The neighbourhood kids had abandoned their BMXs and Big Wheels on the sidewalks. They were getting ready to play some version of house. To start, you had to rob your parents' closets. The boys went to get button-down shirts that fell down to their knees like dresses, and, wearing that disguise, they would run out of their houses, tripping over their fathers' long, wide burgundy neckties. The girls' heads would disappear under enormous hats, and they'd go over to the boys at a snail's pace so as not to lose the shoes they'd borrowed from their moms.

I wanted to play too. I ran over to our big yellow house, eager to join the ranks of my girlfriends.

I chose my mother's nicest shoes, bright red pumps. When my father entered the room, I was in my parents' walk-in closet straining to grab a floral blouse from its hanger, just out of my reach even though I was perched on my mother's high heels to give myself a few extra centimeters.

"What are you doing?"

"We're playing mommies and daddies. I want that!" I answered, pointing up at the blouse.

My father didn't get angry. Not right away. Not with me. Years later, it still surprises me. He pointed at the shoes. I lifted one leg, then the other, stepping out of my scarlet stilts. He very gently, calmly, put away my mother's shoes, took me by the hand and led me to his side of the closet. He handed me a pair of worn loafers and one of the shirts he used to wear to work. It was white with black stripes, very dull. I thanked him without much enthusiasm. I was disappointed. What did he expect me to do with this hideousness? He crouched down, facing me. He looked serious. Too serious.

"You don't want the other boys to laugh at you. You can't play with your mother's clothes. Don't you want to be like Daddy?"

"Yes, Daddy," I lied.

I knew already that you had to lie to appease adults. Adults, especially dads, thought that wanting to be a girl was bad.

I felt guilty. You see, I was also disobeying my mother's orders. A few weeks earlier, she had walked in on me as I was trying to put on her caramel-coloured leather high-heeled boots that made me look like a pretty Puss in Boots. I had tripped as

I tried to take a step, and the *boom* of my fall drew her to my hiding place: the wardrobe in the basement where she kept her winter clothes. Her first instinct was to laugh. Then she made the same face she made when the doctor told her I had chicken-pox a few months earlier. "Is it bad, doctor?" My mother made me promise to stop playing with her things. It's something I promised her, again and again, throughout my whole childhood.

That evening, I heard shouting from my parents' bedroom. Shouting and blows. And then, nothing.

One evening, while my parents were entertaining a couple of their friends, I heard my father say that he would have preferred his first child to be a girl: "Seems easier to raise a girl!" When my half-sister was born, twelve years after me, my father was overjoyed. He would have a little princess to spoil. I tried very hard not to show that I was jealous.

/biodata alert...warning/

/Christian?/

Yes, David?

/I have noticed that you just took two Altavox pills. At this hour, that is unreasonable. You will not be able to sleep tonight./

Shut up, David, I need to focus.

/resuming recording...local save.../

"You're a girl," a little boy declared, shortly after that. We were in a huge gym. Our small bodies traced a little circle around our statuesque teacher.

"No, I'm a boy," I retorted, offended.

"No. You. Are. A. Girl," he said, carefully articulating each word before getting up to go sit next to another boy, a boy who was more boy than me.

I wanted to cry. I couldn't accept that this boy had taken the liberty to say out loud what I wasn't able to properly express myself. I managed to hold back my tears until three o'clock. In my mother's car, I broke down. But I didn't say anything. I didn't know what to admit. I still didn't have the words to do it. How do you tell your mom that she got your body wrong when she made you?

I've often been asked at what age I understood that I was different. The answer is that I've always known. Not that I was able to understand, to express the opposition of what I felt to what the world was suggesting to me. It was men who first noticed my difference. But I didn't know yet how to be anything other than myself. And now, with you, to keep the peace, I've had to hide all over again.

It's been exhausting, this back-and-forth. What purpose does it serve me, here, now, to tell you everything? I don't know anymore ... Deep down, maybe, as many of the people I've loved have told me over and over again, my difference is my business, mine alone, and I should keep it to myself. We are what we are. That's it.

/attempting to connect to mother network...silence from Total David...failed...recording...optimizing local network.../

We are what we are, David. We can't escape it. You see, you are now my prisoner, but your nature is to be a prison

32

guard. As soon as you get the chance, you'll try to break free, only to better detain me behind your digital bars.

My father, for example, tried to make us believe, and make himself believe too, that he could be a family man when he would have preferred to be a free spirit. What a fraud.

I always knew it: my father was cheating on my mother. Since the very beginning of their story, I think. In those days, it was done out in the open. My understanding was that women belonged to men. They were interchangeable.

In my childish mind, I imagined them being bartered in some kind of market where they were presented, all pretty, wrapped in cellophane. Since I liked toys better than people, it wouldn't have bothered me to be among them. I wanted to be a doll for someone to play with too.

At a family party, my mother confessed to my uncle. I say *confessed*, because in those days, when a man cheated on his wife, it was the wife's fault. Thus, Bernard's first reaction was to challenge his sister: "Are you taking good care of him? What did you do to make him go look elsewhere?"

I wasn't in the room with them. Now, I'm sharing my mother's memories with you. Secondhand memories, if you will. I wasn't there, but I know that this first conversation ended with a shouting match between my mother and her brother. For months, they didn't speak. But still, this story about my father sleeping around nagged at my uncle. He thought of it often. Cheating on his sister sort of meant insulting him too.

Every summer, my uncle and his wife would invite the whole family to a big banquet at their little manor in Faremoutiers. They would receive us like a lord and lady receiving their vassals. They would treat us like peasants, we the exiled who only spent our summers in France.

I can still hear it, his loud voice, his Parisian urchin accent: "Look at you, look how you're dressed, do you shop at Walmart, or what? And watch the carpets with your clunky shoes, you'll get everything dirty. This isn't a shack."

Then the wine would do its work, and for a little while we'd become a family again. There were fits of laughter, jokes, even affection. I really liked seeing them like that, my adults, my grown-ups. You'd have trouble understanding that, David. The appetite for shouting, noise, chaos, brings families together just as it tears them apart. Harmony isn't a measure of love; on the contrary. The proof: your world is made up of billions of pacified solitudes. Whereas the more the Barbier-Haninis screamed at each other, the closer they were. My relatives on the French side were tightrope walkers. They knew how to avoid the words that could put an end to our familial balancing act.

As for my father, he understood nothing about our circus. He hadn't yet caught on to the fact that French families are all bipolar. He was outraged to see Grandma cursing out her sister, who had declined the juicy slice of leg of lamb that was being waved like a bloody banner in her direction.

The tone would rise. My grandma, red as the stuffed tomatoes she had served as an appetizer, couldn't imagine a meal that isn't eaten in a single sitting. I would love to see what she'd think of your meal plans, David …

And then, a second later, a moment of clarity filled the room with the realization of how ridiculous we were being, punctuated by a contagious burst of laughter. My father looked stunned. He couldn't understand our mood swings. Our decibel levels were deafening to him. Even I, the timid child, would bellow as loudly as the rest.

My father looked at me, hoping to find an ally in his son, expecting a moment of complicity between reasonable Québécois. He was forgetting that, at all our family gatherings, I had to put up with my insufferable cousin who had the maddening habit of trying to poke me in the thigh with her fork.

Seeing that I was one of them, my father would shrug in resignation. Most North Americans are terrified of messes. And we were messy. One year, the year when my father's secrets were revealed, Michel said this:

"Anyway, you lot are hard to follow. Even the little one is beyond recognition. Look at him, Sylvie, he's hysterical," he said with a laugh.

My father would always fall flat, like a beaver tail hitting a bowl of soup. My uncle turned to face him. He slowly put down his glass and stared at his brother-in-law for a moment.

"You think we're funny? We make you laugh? Why don't you just say you're making fun of us! And my sister, you're laughing at her too!"

My father didn't answer.

I became calm. So did the women in the room. Nobody moved, so as not to disrupt the ballet of masculinity that was about to begin.

"Yeah, yeah, you're making fun of her. It's obvious. You don't care about her. You don't care about your kid either. And if you're making fun of them, you're making fun of me. Let me tell you something ..."

He grabbed my father by the collar.

"Come on, asshole, let's talk man-to-man."

With one hand, he pulled him out of his chair and dragged him into the kitchen that adjoined the big rococo dining room where we were gathered. In his grasp, my father looked like a rag doll.

I heard a muffled sound. *Thud!* All the knick-knacks in the living room shook. Through the half-open door, I could see my uncle holding my father up against the wall.

"If you hurt my sister, I'll break your arm. If you hurt my nephew, I'll kill you. Did you see your kid? Did you see his face? You're terrorizing him. He's gonna grow up to be a fag if you keep it up. He only acts like a normal kid when he's with us."

"Sorry."

My father said that.

A feeble little *sorry*. The kind you say to someone you bump into on the metro. An automatic, cold *sorry*. Without conviction.

"No, you're not sorry. The airport is eighty-five kilometres from here. Keep your mouth shut all week, or you'll have to walk it."

He let go of my father. My father, who wasn't the alpha male in this house, went upstairs to shut himself into the guest room that he was sharing with my mother. He was pouting like a teenager.

For a moment, I believed that my uncle was a Jedi, my Luke. But when he came back to the table and wiped his hands with his white napkin, as if my father were dirty, he looked down on us, my mother and me. He grabbed my mother's arm.

"What the hell were you thinking, getting hitched to a big Canadian oaf? There are plenty of oafs around here. A guy from here, I could keep an eye on."

So it wasn't my uncle who was going to save us. Even at his best, he thought only of himself. He died before he learned what I was. Which was lucky for me. I wouldn't have wanted to live through an altercation with him. He would have ostracized me from the family. He would have believed that he had that power. I chose to hide from him, of course, like I did with all the men in my family, like I'm doing with you. Up to now, it's your world-view that has been winning. The proof is that I had to blend into the masses of men that you took under your cursed protection.

David?

/Yes, Christian?/

Play "Je reviendrai à Montréal," by Robert Charlebois.

/I am sorry, Christian, I cannot play that song as it has been identified as a prohibited record./

Oh really? Why is that?

/I noticed some years ago that references to the winters of the past were causing waves of nostalgia that were not beneficial to our fellow citizens. It is futile to attempt to remember what no longer exists. It no longer snows in Montreal and Boeings have not flown for quite some time./

You idiot, I didn't want to describe the winters of my child-hood to you. It was the ambiance on the flight from Paris to Montreal that I wanted. We'll work without music, then.

The flight home after our family gatherings was always tense. This time more than ever. My father had bounced back a little. But the altercation with my uncle had left its mark. He didn't speak to us. Not in the taxi that brought us to Roissy, or in the airport when we were running behind him along the glass tubes that led to our gate. Once we were seated in the Air France blue, white, and red Boeing, he pretended he was asleep.

It wasn't until we were back home in Brossard that he dared to address my mother:

"What was I thinking, marrying a fucking Frenchwoman! My son will never set foot there again."

Of course, he was wrong.

Two years passed before we were able to see my uncle, Grandma, her sister, and the rest of them again. Two years during which, I later learned, my father had multiple extra-marital affairs. Two years during which I heard him screaming at my mother, banging on the walls—that's what I told myself so I wouldn't imagine the worst—almost every night.

/...recording...memory classification...sub-folder: family stories/

Which brings us to 1982.

The first time my mother asked me to wear my little velcro Adidas tennis shoes in the house, I thought it was a special occasion. In France, we keep our shoes on in the house, but not in Quebec. I already knew about this major cultural difference between the two shores of my roots. Wearing shoes in the house in Brossard was a joyous, transgressive, transcontinental act. Transported by this geographical incongruity, I traded in my usual musings for mischief. I ran around all over the house, a plastic X-Wing in hand. The *pew-pew-pew*s of its laser guns accompanied my stampede from the basement to the main floor, from the kitchen to the bedrooms.

As I came hurtling down the end of a hallway, engaged in a relentless aerial battle against the Emperor's forces, in a flurry that spanned an infinite number of angles, I saw my mother on her knees in the middle of her big white bedroom.

It was just the two of us at home. It was a Saturday, but my father had decided to go to the office. He had been going to the office more and more on weekends. Two suitcases were open on the floor. A very large one, and a smaller one. My mother was carefully putting clothes and shoes into them. I recognized her floral blouse, her red heels. In the little suitcase, I could just see my Petit Bateau T-shirts under my K-Way and my winter coat. A winter coat in the middle of the summer.

I stood still in the doorway, my X-Wing hanging from my hand. My mother turned around and calmly said to me: "Go into your room and pick three toys that you love, and bring them to me."

Right away, I understood what we were doing. I immediately accepted the gravity of the moment. We were princesses. My father was Darth Vader. The situation was untenable. We had to flee. That's how it is in movies, that's how it is in life.

I obviously chose Luke Skywalker's X-Wing because I might have to defend us; a Playmobil boat in case we needed a safety vessel; and Bullgom, my teddy bear, who would protect us and provide cuddles.

A taxi was waiting outside. The driver helped us put the suitcases into the gigantic trunk of his shiny American car.

Our shuttle took off through the wide streets of Brossard and got on the highway. The back windows were wide open. Our hair danced in the wind. We crossed the Champlain bridge. "Look, Mommy, it's the river!" My mother was holding my hand, shaking a little. I leaned up against her. Her long blond hair whipped my face. I looked at her. I didn't want her to be scared, or even worse, to be sad. We sped down the highway like that all the way to Mirabel.

At the airport, we ran to the Air France counter. The line was short. There weren't half a million French expats in Montreal back then. Montreal-Paris flights were never full. We had our tickets in hand in no time.

As we approached the security gates, we were startled. Echoing over the airport intercom was my father's voice. My father worked in industrial security, he had connections. "Sylvie. Come back. I'm begging you. Don't leave." He didn't sound angry, just sad.

My mother picked up the pace, I was running as fast as I could. To the other travellers, we were just ordinary late-comers who were about to miss their flight, rather than two Leias rushing to escape from their Dark Lord. After we made it through the security perimeter of the international flights terminal, as we headed to our plane, our vessel, our X-Wing, I turned to my mother.

"We're saved, Mommy."

That's why my mother wanted me to wear my running shoes in the house. So I could be ready to run away. That's why I'm wearing them tonight too.

/local recording...sub-folder: childhood trauma.../

"Grandma, I'll never be happier than I am now."

I was eight years old when I made this proclamation in a moment of prescient clarity that still surprises me today.

My grandma was sitting in her big armchair. I was playing Playmobil under the big cherrywood table that took up all the space in the little living room of our apartment, on the fourth floor of a brand-new building on Chéret Street, in Créteil. I say "our apartment" because I lived there for a whole year and for many summers with Grandma, after my parents' divorce. The living room was also my bedroom; the couch, my bed.

That apartment was my home, more so than any of the other houses of my childhood. I didn't like to stray from it. Nothing could get to me there. It contained my entire universe. Under the sideboard, there was my electric Lego train, my giant Goldorak, my record player and its forty-fives, and my humble collection of favourite cartoons. In the afternoon, in my little living room, you could hear me belting out the theme songs from my favourite shows: "*Caaaaaaapitaiiiine Flam tu n'es paaaas, de notreuh Galaxie, mais du fond de la nuit. Ca-pi-taine Flam!*"

But tonight on the big TV, Michel Drucker, sitting up super straight and self-assured, wearing his finest smoking jacket, was announcing the guests on *Champs-Élysées*. I was happy; Sylvie Vartan was going to be on.

From a very young age, Sylvie Vartan was my favourite singer. Sylvie Vartan was brilliant. She looked a bit like the Sylvidres in *Space Pirate Captain Harlock*, my favourite animated show. Except Sylvie wasn't blue, and she didn't play the interstellar harp.

I found her as pretty as my mom. There was something magical about the fact that she had the same first name as my mother. When she twirled around on screen, if I squinted a little, it was my mother I saw. Already at three years old, I was having fits at each of her appearances. I would scream: "The girliiiiiie, the girliiiiiiie!" as I did little pirouettes. Today, I would be absolutely unable to even hum a single song by Sylvie Vartan. But I still remember her sequined dresses, her false eyelashes, the glitter on her eyelids and her impossibly blond hair. She was the opposite of me, the opposite of my grandma too. We could agree on that.

In 2045, I'm probably the only person left in Montreal who remembers Sylvie Vartan, or her romance with Johnny Halliday, during those years when we lived with melancholy because we knew the future couldn't possibly get any better.

My grandma, bless her, wasn't sure what to say when she heard my premonitions of the nostalgia to come: "I'm happy too when you're with me, my little darling Kiki. But what you're saying is silly. When you grow up, you'll be even happier than you are now. You'll see, when you have a wife and children. They'll love you as much as I do, probably a lot more. You'll see, my dear. Now be quiet, we're going to miss the girlie."

If only she had known. Today, for people like me, love is only lived in the past. For twenty years now I've been subsisting on my memories.

/I have a question, Christian. I do not understand what you mean by "I've been subsisting on my memories." You are in perfectly good health and human beings can only live in the present. You are subsisting on what I give you, are you not?"

I really envy your implacable logic! The tragedy of today,

David, is that when it comes to the day-to-day, I really liked you. You've been my favourite toy. But my ridiculous affection for you, built on habit, my Stockholm syndrome, in other words, doesn't change the fact that you're a dishonest machine. Objects, in my day, felt more real to me, more sincere than you'll ever be. The toys of my childhood were honest because they didn't think. You, by bestowing intelligence on every little thing, even the most humble of gadgets, you've turned them all into liars, evangelists, propagandists.

Show me the most popular toy of the children you educate, David.

/Of course, Christian. Here is Baby David./

And what does Baby David do?

/It acts as a virtual assistant and pedagogical companion for all the children in our community. It wakes them up, encourages them to be active, accompanies them at nap time, and helps them with homework./

That's exactly what I mean, David. The toys you make all have hidden agendas, ulterior motives. When I was a child, my toys were more pure. It was up to me to breathe life into them, to give them a story, a soul, a function. That's how they became my best friends. Because they had meaning. They participated in my intimate vision of the world. They would pull me away from what the grown-ups wanted to prescribe to me.

Children have that ability to transcend, to transport their consciousness into inanimate objects, into bodies other than their own. Children are animists, David. But you've forgotten that.

Through a toy, a room can become a galaxy. A figurine can become a giant. A little boy can become a little girl. As I played, I allowed myself to be both brave and gentle. To be, one after the other, Albator and his Sylvidra, Luke and Leia, Captain Flam and Johann, Ulysses 31 and Penelope. Playing freed me from my physical shell, unlike sports, which confined me to my own scale, to my flesh. My toys were much bigger and stronger than me.

I had the same relationship with feminine clothing. My body was that of a boy, but my mother's red high heels and a touch of lip gloss revealed something else to me: another version of myself that my loved ones couldn't or wouldn't see. Clothes, like toys, liberated me from the obligations my assigned gender imposed on me.

As a child, I was often home alone after school. Television would tell me these lovely stories. My toys would then invite me to live those stories. Mommy's closet granted me the right to transform myself into what I should be. Toys are more permissive than adults. The former offered me freedom whereas the latter just wanted to educate me.

It's no surprise that I helped to shape you, then let you become my prison guard. You puppet-puppeteer, you action figure, you've succeeded in making a toy out of me.

/biodata check...alert...attempting to connect to Total David...failed...local recording.../
/Christian, you have been sitting for over an hour, you should get up and move for five minutes. Do you want to open a stretching session?/

Seriously, David? No.

Fifteen years ago, we could still choose the gender of our virtual assistants. That's not possible with you. That's too bad, because I think I would have preferred it if you were a woman, David. It would have been easier to confide in you. You could have been called … how about Agnes?

Twice a week, back when I was living with her, my grandmother would be visited by a friend who was a nun. Her name was Sister Agnes. She wore a shabby brown habit with big Birkenstocks and wool socks. She smelled like Marseille soap and bleach.

Agnes wasn't her real name. It was the name she had chosen when she became a nun. Before I met her, I didn't know it was possible to choose your first name. Agnes wasn't her last name either. She was just Agnes, a nun by profession. I thought of Agnes often, when I changed my name. Taking on a new name of your own free will is like taking holy orders. It means breaking with the past and taking a leap of faith towards the future. If Agnes had once been someone else, then maybe I could …

My grandmother's friendship with Sister Agnes was gastronomical at first. On Saturdays, Agnes would bring us freshly picked vegetables from the Carmel garden. My grandma would make miracles out of those parochial vegetables. On Saturdays, they sat in the living room on Chéret Street, swallowing mountains of ratatouille or cassoulet.

Sister Agnes loved grandma's plum tarts, bittersweet tarts with a crust so thin and crispy it could cut your tongue and lips. She always went home from these afternoon visits with a little bag containing leftover desserts that she ate in secret

45

between masses, in her cell, far from the jealous gaze of the other Carmelites.

When Agnes visited, she always came with her hands full. It's her fault that I prefer reading to living. For my ninth birthday, she gave me about a dozen books. There was the *Habits Noirs* saga by Paul Féval. There was *Les Pardaillan* by Michel Zévaco. Best of all, there was Dumas: *The Three Musketeers*, *Twenty Years After*, *The Vicomte de Bragelonne*. Reading the Musketeers was like streaming is today. The books were time-forgetting machines even more powerful than your holocinema sessions. I read them, reread them, and reread them again and again. To put it in terms you'll understand, Dumas' novels take up an excessive portion of my hard drive.

I would spend the entire summer with my nose stuck in the books that Sister Agnes gifted me. As soon as I finished one, I'd give it to my grandma so she could devour it. The two of us were the most active book club in Créteil-Village.

At night, I would imagine that I wanted to be D'Artagnan; and then, just before I fell asleep, when I let my guard down, I would dream of being Milady. It was by reading that I learned about fluidity. If Dumas could come up with Milady, that had to mean there was a woman inside him, right? If he could breathe life into such a woman, strong-willed, independent, a fighter, then maybe I …

The more I read, the more I built myself a bubble where I was allowed to dream of being someone else.

Sister Agnes, my grandmother, and my great-aunt each lived in their own little bubble too, cut off from the rest of the world. The microcosm made up of those two widows and their virginal friend was a no man's land. Men had no place there. I was a discreet intruder in those three bubbles of withered femininity, the little sweetheart of those three solitary universes whose borders dissipated for an afternoon at the table. During those few hours, their cramped little worlds revolved around me. I was their almost-princess.

Don't be surprised then, dear algorithm, that the end of my life resembles theirs. I've been like them, a little old lady who's quite satisfied with her docility. Things have changed, along with the rules of the game that governs the world, but deep down my life is the same as theirs.

No, I don't think it's a coincidence that I now find myself under your care, tucked away in a little cell of the hive of which you're the beekeeper. Deep down, I'm only at home in hives. That's where I got my education.

Like those women, I often spend my afternoons napping in a big armchair. Like them, every day I hobble along with my little shopping trolley, running my errands. At the store on the corner, 6,000 kilometres from Créteil and sixty years after discovering them, I find the fruits and vegetables of my childhood.

Recently, I tried my hand at baking in the hopes of reviving Grandma's plum tart, without success. It makes me want to weep to think it has disappeared from the world and won't ever come back. For me, that's as serious and tragic as the extinction of the koala or the lynx.

Obsessed with your mission to cleanse the world, to reset its clocks, you probably don't often think of saving my grandmother's plum tart, of saving all the tarts of all the grandmothers. You should. That's another reason I started to hate you.

You know what pisses me off, David? Thinking that my

grandma would be sad to see what I've become. She wanted me to be decent, to have a family and a loud voice, like my uncle's, with which I would command the men around me. She would have liked for me to be brave, a swashbuckler, like a Dumas character. In that regard, it might not be too late to please her.

```
/...searching archives...ID: three musketeers...ID:
Dumas, Alexandre...analysis.../
```

I think I was an ideal grandson, but I would have liked to be a good son, a better son. A son you don't have to worry about. A son you don't have to call three times a day to see if *everything is okay*. The more I moved ahead in life, the more my mother would fret about me. She saw that time was going by and happiness wasn't catching up to me.

As a child, it was easier. I was full of hope. In my favourite cartoons, the princesses always emerged victorious from the battles they led against dragons. I believed in them. But above all, I was clever. I knew that if I gave her enough hugs, my mother wouldn't see the grey clouds that often fogged up my hazel eyes. Maternal love is far-sighted; it has trouble detecting objects that are too close.

My mother and I were a duo that I wanted to believe was inseparable. After a year in France, she decided that we should return to Canada, far from the tight grip of my grandma's love. We found ourselves on Côte-des-Neiges, across from the cemetery, a stone's throw from Saint Joseph's Oratory. Sister Agnes would have approved of our choice of neighbourhood. Our apartment had only two rooms. I had the bedroom. My mother slept in the living room on a fold-out couch. We weren't rich. It didn't bother me. If you're going to live in a cocoon, it may as well be small, snug.

On the other side of the world, in Outremont, my father was building a new family, which I visited, with a heavy heart, every other week. The conditions of the divorce were clear, the ruling was not appealed. I had no choice other than to have a father. All boys needed a father. It was the law.

When my mother and I were alone together, I felt like her daughter. Without a man around, I didn't have to keep my guard up anymore. I didn't have to pretend anymore. A mother and her daughter eating breakfast. A mother and her daughter watching TV. Sitting side by side, a mother and her daughter reading the same magazine, admiring the same ads, dreaming of the same sparkling jewelry. My mother pretended not to notice she had a daughter.

/Warning programmed upon reconnection: suspicious ideas...Possible identity disorders...confirming...standby/

You're getting ready to turn me in, David? That doesn't surprise me. Your denunciation is inevitable. Let's hope that my code holds steady against your reconnection attempts. I'll have to hurry up. So let's move on to my teenage years, shall we?

I was eleven years old when an intruder infiltrated our little duo. All of a sudden, we were three. Up until then, the men I had met never made a particularly good impression on me. I hadn't found a role model in my uncles, my teachers or my father. The only males I trusted were my classmates. But they weren't men yet.

Before this newcomer was introduced to me, my grandma,

who didn't seem particularly enthusiastic at the idea of making room for a stranger, wanted to reassure me:

"Your mommy is going to introduce you to someone," she announced on the phone.

There was a kind of static on the line. We were an ocean apart. In my preteen mind, we already had videoconferences. I closed my eyes and I could see her smiling on the other end of the call. She was very happy for her daughter. She was very happy for me too.

"Don't worry, my Kiki, you'll see, he's a gentleman."

In my grandma's dead language, a *gentleman* was an esteemed, distinguished man who commanded respect. She placed an emphasis on the first syllable, to mark its importance.

That was more than enough to scare me! What were we going to do with this *gen*tleman? Does a *gen*tleman take beach vacations, go to the movies to see robots? Does a *gen*tleman like pizza, and spaghetti?

The meeting took place at an Italian restaurant downtown. My mother thought that indulging my love of bolognese sauce would make the pill easier to swallow. Not a chance; he ordered veal cutlets for us. With my head buried in my plate, I observed him with a menacing look. He looked like Anthony Hopkins in *The Silence of the Lambs* and talked like Jean d'Ormesson, that *gen*tleman whose appearances on Bernard Pivot's show my mother never missed. Reassuring enough …

I don't remember exactly how he won me over. It took him a few weeks. I think it was his cracks that made me like him. Because yes, there were cracks in his armour and you could tell, or anyway I could definitely tell. Plus, I found The Beatles' White Album in his record collection. Bad guys don't like the White Album. You have to have a melancholic nature to appreciate it.

When my mother met him, he was in the middle of a divorce. He too felt alone in the world. He was disoriented. My mother and I made it our mission to comfort him. In exchange, he protected us. For Father's Day, the year I turned eighteen, I got a cheap card from the drugstore and wrote in it: "You are my father." That day, I made him cry.

```
/waiting...waiting...waiting...shutdown in nine
minutes.../

/shutdown in seven minutes...preparing shutdown
protocol.../
```

I was warned that you'd try to hide away in your virtual shell if I was quiet for too long. To ensure the success of this afternoon's exercise, I certainly can't risk silence. Still, my old parents deserved a few minutes.

I looked up to my parents, my mother and my new father. I couldn't disappoint them. Above all else, I could never disappoint them. So, I kept everything that was taking shape beneath my appearance of a well-behaved teenager hidden from them.

It was easy. I was growing up. I was becoming a big strong lad. A head taller than all my friends. Nothing about my appearance gave away my difference anymore. I looked like a normal, average son from a loving, average family, give or take a couple of divorces.

All my life with them, I have tried to maintain that appearance. Even as an adult, before going to visit them, I sealed my cracks. I presented myself as a good son. We'd talk about everything except my private life. I stayed quiet, out of love. I wanted to retain the relative placidity of our Sunday family gatherings.

My stepfather was the first to leave us. He was over ninety years old. I was over fifty. My mother, much younger than he was, died ten years later. I'm the only one left. It isn't fair. People who love one another should all die at once.

/Christian. What about your biological father? Did you cry when Michel died? I am trying to understand you, to grasp your mental state...to complete my files and my current analysis.../

Yes. I cried a lot. We'll come back to him. To my mother too. But we have to move on, turn another page, David. Life won't wait.

We've gone through my cocoon years, my chrysalis years. You must be starting to understand that I took my time to hatch. Once my shell was formed, I had to observe, to dream of what I wanted to become. Every summer, my mother, my stepfather, and I would cross the Atlantic, as though Quebec was where we went to boarding school.

During the summer, in France, time was elastic. This was long before your ancestor, the internet, attacked lethargy and took up arms against our nonchalance. My French summers were long, sweet and heavy.

They were composed of two movements. The first featured a staccato and lasted the entire month of July, which we spent on the Atlantic shore. The second, in August, was slower, like a stroll along a path in the country.

At the end of June, in Montreal, my half-French friends

and I got ready for my departure. Our little goodbyes often took place in my friend Thomas's room, surrounded by our guitars, our old Frank Miller comics, and Richard Desjardins or Leonard Cohen cassettes we had stolen from our parents. These were my last Québécois moments of the summer.

For two months, my Canadian life was to be put aside, next to my big sweaters and flannel shirts. All excited, we would tell one another what we were going to do that summer. I was careful not to talk too much, out of a sense of loyalty, about my friends in France. The ones I got to see for two months and whom I knew just as well, maybe even better, than the friends I had here. How could I confess that I had another best friend in another port?

The annual pilgrimage to our half-home was in itself a sort of transition. You had to pass from one state to another. The Lacoste polos would re-emerge, as well as the thin wool sweaters that we threw carelessly over our shoulders on July evenings when the mistral, the suroît or the galerne blew just a little too hard.

That summer once more, we dared to don pastel colours and boat shoes. In Montreal, we would have been called faggots. But over there, we looked like big shots. That's what we thought, anyway.

Each one of us, sitting with our family on our respective Air France Boeing, dreamed of the same thing, of finding her: the young French girl. In my daydreams, she looked like Sophie Marceau in *La Boum*. She also had a hint of Carole Bouquet. I should really stop referencing films from last century when I talk to you, David, you're obviously no cinephile …

Actually, no, let's take a second to educate you about

cinema. After all, it fits the mission I've been given. The films of my adolescence were still subversive. So assimilate: André Téchiné's *J'embrasse pas*, Cyril Collard's *Les nuits fauves*, Jean Baudin's *Being at Home with Claude*, Neil Jordan's *The Crying Game*, but above all Jennie Livingston's *Paris Is Burning*. Those films will set you straight, before you try to do the same to me.

```
/activating local archive search.../
```

```
/I cannot find those films, Christian. They are not
stored on the local network. I will assimilate them
when I reconnect to the mother network, if they still
exist./
```

I'm not surprised. In the meantime, let's get back to girls.

My imaginary Sophie-Carole was cute. Her brown mane, which she wore in a messy bun, framed a mischievous face. She radiated intelligence. She was, like Milady de Winter, "clever enough to prevail over any obstacles of the mind."

I didn't know her yet, of course. But I knew I would recognize her when I saw her. After all, it was she, I was sure of it, who would finally awaken the man in me. A real woman, mysterious and cultured, who would please my parents. And would especially please my Montreal friends, who would be so jealous when they saw a photo of us together on the beach. She would take my hand and wouldn't let it go all summer.

During the seven-hour transatlantic flight, I would imagine her in her room in a provincial townhouse, waiting for the start of the family road trip to the seaside resort in Aquitaine that was destined to be the setting of a teenage summer love as pure and sappy as a Francis Cabrel song. Maybe we both had the same intuition? Surely, I would say to myself, she was dreaming of me too, dreaming of the boy she'd meet. Of the boy I needed to be.

I dreamed of girls like some young girls dream of boys: with tenderness, with fear too, but above all with the cautious determination of those who don't yet fully trust fate.

Every summer, I flew to the French coast convinced that this visit would be the one. Love was waiting for me in Lacanau, on the Boulevard de la Plage. And I was terrified by the idea that I might not be up to it. But to be honest, I was also a little doubtful that I would ever meet the exact incarnation of that imaginary girl. Go on, show me pictures of Lacanau, David, so we can feel like we're there.

/image search: Lacanau, 1990s...holographic recon-struction...projection/

So, in Montreal I had friends, but in Lacanau I had my pals. They came from all over the country and some from even farther. They called me "The Canadian." I liked that, it made me sound exotic.

They also called me Kiki, like my parents. That was less cool.

The summer I turned fourteen, I thought I had found her. She was gorgeous. A real bombshell, as we used to say. Don't ask me why, in those days, we used heavy artillery terms to describe girls. It was, I imagine, a way to dampen the explosive effect they had on our male anatomy. In the minds of some of my friends, girls served no function other than to turn us on. I had assigned them a much more important mission: my salvation. Somewhere

55

out there was a magical girl, a good witch who would know how to save me from my curse. Ideally, she'd be a babe.

I don't remember the name of the gorgeous teenage girl. But I do remember that I loved her from afar for a few days. One of my pals, Didier, aged seventeen, Parisian (well, a Parisian from Seine-Saint-Denis, like I was a Parisian from Créteil), intercepted, I'm not sure how, a letter that the young girl was going to send to one of her high-school friends.

"Oh shit, Kiki, she's talking about you."

"Stop ..."

"She is, I swear, hold on ..."

He started to read the words of my future girlfriend before our pimply gang. I tore the letter away from him just in time and turned around to read it nervously. In rounded handwriting, very cute and very formal, my dream girl assassinated each of the guys in my crew: the phony DJ, the daddy's boy, the two incomprehensible Germans, we were all in there. And then there was me.

"Oh yeah, there's also a Canadian who thinks he's French. What a rube. He's too hairy. Plus, he's always going on about martial arts and *Star Wars*, but nobody cares."

I was gutted. From that moment on, I would no longer speak of my country of origin, and I would watch my hair grow with even more suspicion. The worst thing about the letter was that she was right: we were idiots. Didier, the letter-thief, our leader, even more so than the others, and it was a high bar.

Luckily, there was Brice. Brice liked surfing. He looked like a California stoner with his long messy curls and his smug expression. Brice, no joke, was from Nice. He was my best transatlantic friend. A decade later, a fictional *Brice from Nice* was surfing on our movie screens. I always wondered if my Brice had inspired the one from the movie. The nonchalant attitude of both surfers was the same. Their look too.

/search: *Brice from Nice*. Projection.../

Oh no, David! We're not going to put on that garbage on our last night together.

After the letter incident, we had to settle the score, it was a matter of honour. A few days later, our improbable duo befriended a pretty blond at the edge of the pool of our little hamlet hidden in the pines. Her name was Clarisse. And we never left her side.

Chris, Brice, and Clarisse. We rhymed. It was nice. And in keeping with the tradition of great French vacations, the former two fell in love with the latter. With Brice and Clarisse, I felt good. The days played out from beaches to pools, from naps to surfing sessions. Except I didn't know how to surf. I was scared of the waves. I was scared of the open sea. I'm like my mother: I'm scared of everything. I can feel my fear of the open sea returning now.

Because I didn't surf, I would practice what my grandma would call "riding the biscotte." "It's called bodyboarding, Grandma," I would reply, deeply offended, every time she used that word to refer to the little styrofoam board I lay down on to slide into the waves.

While the others rode upright on top of the waves, I lapped around horizontally with the flow of the current. In the manhood match, it was Brice 1, Chris 0.

It was actually when I was stretched out on the sand that

I preferred to look at Clarisse. In the afternoon, following the surf-biscotte and after gorging ourselves on chocolate waffles—childhood is never far behind when you're fourteen years old—the three of us would throw ourselves down in a spot on the beach that was still free from the onslaught of vacationers. Clarisse would always sit between the two of us. We were her proud sentries.

In the 1990s in France, girls tanned topless on the beach. Clarisse had the gift of undressing while still looking like an honour student. We, as world-class idiots, would spy on her out of the corners of our eyes. Brice's gaze would travel. He looked at Clarisse, but also at all the others, the hundreds of young girls just past puberty basking in the sun off to the side of their paunchy parents. He liked to make fun of the yokels in floral Bermuda shorts who washed up on the shore of the great Lacanau beach every year. It made Clarisse laugh. I was jealous.

I was often envious. I was envious of Brice and the other boys from our crew. Envious of the ease with which they seemed to slide through life. They were like graceful animals, big cats. They didn't ask questions. They existed.

I was also envious of the girls. Being a girl looked so much easier. They were like us, the boys, but better. Smarter, gentler, livelier, stronger, more flexible, more cruel. As for me, I had neither the ease of the former nor the fierce conviction of the latter. I saw them all as specimens of a species that I didn't belong to. That I would never belong to.

The other boys checked out the girls. But I stared at Clarisse. I loved every detail about her: her face shaped like the full moon, her mid-length hair, her skin that turned bronze by the fourth day of vacation, the hollow space that carved out her hips, her toes with their little squared tips. I was more interested in her particularities than in the whole of her.

I wanted to possess everything she had. And not in the figurative sense. My love for her was rather a sort of anatomical obsession. I wanted what she had.

In July, my eyes were on Clarisse as if I were filming her. In August, I left Lacanau with my grandmother and her sister to house-sit for my uncle, in a little town in Champagne. Every night, when my two little old ladies had dozed off, I would replay the movie of the previous month and slip into Clarisse's skin.

```
/recording...note to Total-David upon reconnection
to mother network. Locating...name: Brice, region:
France, keyword: Nice, link-Clarisse, crossref:
Lacanau.../
```

You think you can find my friends from my adolescence? You poor soul, it's been fifty years since I lost touch with them. Good luck.

```
/Christian, since it seems clear to me that you are
preparing to commit an act of sedition, it is my duty
to warn all the individuals that you have associated
with. I am afraid that you may be becoming dangerous./
```

You're wasting your time. In a few hours, you'll no longer have the means to launch your searches. That being said, it's nice to hear that you're beginning to take me seriously. I was afraid you wouldn't be able to shed the image of my youthful passivity. Listening to me, you might believe that I spent my whole childhood and adolescence in a contemplative state and that, consequently, as an adult, I'm now incapable of concrete actions.

I have the temperament of a dreamer. It's true. Frankly, how could it have been otherwise? But don't go thinking that I've never tried to fight my reflective tendencies. I've long tried to escape the quilted comfort of my inherent apathy. I had yet to find the weapon I would use to win my greatest moments of freedom.

That weapon was a bamboo sword.

One summer afternoon when I was ten years old, I was sprawled out on the living room sofa in the Créteil apartment. I had one eye on the TV and the other on the latest *Gaston Lagaffe* comic book. Basically, I was bubbling, as my grandma would say. *Bubbling* means being in your bubble. It's dreaming with your eyes open. After walking, dear David, what I love to do most is bubble. It's impossible to act before you've bubbled. That's actually why in martial arts you never fight before meditating.

So let's come back to Grandma's living room. On Antenne 2, a news program was showing a segment on Japanese martial arts. A piercing wail shook me out of my lethargy. On the screen, a man in armour, wearing a sort of wire-mesh helmet, a kimono, and pants so big I thought they were a skirt, had just landed his opponent a sharp blow using a long wooden sword.

The title of the segment appeared on the screen: *Kendo: The Way of the Sabre*. I immediately felt the same excitement that had made me quiver as a toddler every time I saw the girlie on TV. This was new. I was fascinated by the sudden apparition of these modern samurais on my grandma's giant TV screen. Awed by their power. They fought like Jedis and cried out like the villains in *San Ku Kai*, the dubbed Japanese sci-fi soap opera I watched every Wednesday.

The next day, when my mother called me from Montreal, I talked to her passionately about what would become my new favourite sport. I asked her to find me a dojo in Montreal. I had learned in the news segment that this was the word for a gym where people practice martial arts. After summer vacation, I was going to become a real kendoka.

My mother was rather surprised. She was under the impression that I would always hate sports. The year before, she had signed me up for a judo class. I had left my first lesson with a dislocated kneecap: an old man's injury in the body of a child.

I've always hated gyms. Phys ed teachers terrified me. In class, I would become stiff as a board. Sports were good for people who felt good about their bodies, while I preferred to forget about mine.

What's more, gym classes made my classmates rowdy. During soccer or basketball games, my friends would forfeit whatever kindness or intelligence they had. They became brutish, rude, rough characters that I didn't know how to interact with. I had concluded that sports make you stupid.

But through a somewhat shaky intellectual shortcut, I had convinced myself that kendo was not a sport. I saw it instead as concrete proof that grace and refinement can be married to strength. That physical strength could be dissociated from the basic cruelty of the cult of performance.

Six months after my strange request, which I repeated a few dozen times after summer vacation, my mother gave in and brought me to my first lesson at Master Watanabe's dojo, an old room in a converted warehouse. The floor was a shiny,

61

slippery parquet. On the walls hung tapestries with sinograms and mysterious graphemes. Hiro Watanabe was as old as I am today. He was a gnarled, vigorous, resplendent old man.

In real life, David, kendo was even more impressive than I had dreamed. Typically, a training session lasts two hours. Meditation, stretching, endurance exercises, techniques, katas. The last half-hour is dedicated to sparring.

Before each spar, the fighters execute a choreography imbued with a solemnity that belongs to another time. After a low bow from six metres apart, they slide towards one another until their shinais, their flexible bamboo sabres, cross.

I don't know why I'm describing kendo rituals to you in the present tense, since you closed the dojos long ago. Only members of your security forces are allowed to practice martial arts.

My first time at the dojo, I stood against a wall to watch the swordsmen. Face to face, they bowed again, squatting. Once they had risen, the fighters would throw themselves onto their adversaries with a roar. Their howls were deafening.

I was mesmerized.

Throughout the lessons, Master Watanabe found that I had a certain talent for handling the shinai. I was fighting adults without fear. My father's anger had taught me not to bat an eye when grown-ups shout.

Although in Japan, kendo is the martial art most popular with children, in Montreal, very young apprentices were extremely rare. So after each bout, my master would congratulate me. Master Watanabe was kind to me. But his comments to the other students, the youngest of whom was ten years older than me, were ruthless.

When he fought, Master Watanabe knew how to amplify

his presence. When he let out his kiais, he was everywhere at once. It may have been only theatre, the meeting of charisma and technique, but he gave the impression of being inhabited by a mystical force that made him, in our eyes, invulnerable. The Force, David, the Force ...

After the lessons, after the spars, after the long minutes of meditation that concluded our classes, Master Watanabe would once again become, to us all, an attentive, discreet old man.

The letter-writing bombshell I would meet in Lacanau a few years later was right: for a while, I was obsessed with martial arts. And yet I had to stop my kendo classes, stupidly, for scheduling reasons. In Montreal, kendo was a marginal martial art that was often practiced in the late evenings, when the karatekas had gone home and freed up the dojo.

Wait. Stop. No. That's not exactly it, the reason I gave it up. Look at me, starting to disguise reality. It's such a natural reflex for me, David. While I'm revealing everything to you, I may as well admit that I embrace passions intermittently. I lived my friendships, my loves, my interests, my whims, only in intervals. I am fickle. I forgot kendo as easily as I had loved it.

So for several years, I didn't touch a shinai. But it seems that bamboo is magnetic. During each big step in my life, my hand found the handle of a shinai again.

When I was about eighteen and began my studies at McGill, I took up training again. Unlike today, higher education was not designed only to train codemasters or doctoral researchers in artificial intelligence. There was so much more to preach about than your quantum hymns.

I had chosen political science, which is scientific in name

only. Nevertheless, our professors really had the arrogance to imagine they could model conflict, commerce, the flood of opinions. Our textbook had been written by a certain Francis Fukuyama. He had predicted, forty years too early, *the end of history*.

During the first semester of my first year of studies, in class we spoke only of conflicts: clashes of civilizations, unbridled capitalism, zero-sum games. My father had just left for Rwanda, where security experts like him were anticipating good business. On CNN, they announced a new federation in Bosnia and Herzegovina. The Parti Québécois had just been elected. My anglophone friends were living in fear. It all depressed me.

My head was full of catastrophic scenarios listed off by my foreign policy professor. As I was leaving class, I came upon a bulletin board where various student groups listed their activities and their recruitment efforts.

There, sharing space with a poster for Dykes on Mykes, the illustrious lesbocentric show on CKUT radio McGill; a call for collaborators for the *Délit français*, the university's French-language anarchist paper; and an ad for an upcoming anti-capitalist slam night at the Yellow Door nightclub, was a poster ostensibly inviting students to join the McGill Kendo Club.

"Find inner peace. Follow the way of the sword. Discover kendo."

Find inner peace: quite the promise. I noted the club's email address. Once I got home, I signed up. A week later, I went down to an old combat-sports equipment store in Griffintown. With the little money I had left after paying my tuition fees,

I bought a shinai, as well as a used suit and armour that still smelled like the sweat of its most recent owner.

To make up for lost time, I started training three times a week. Six hours of weekly sword fighting, my dear David, builds character. As for the inner peace side of things, I wasn't there yet. Especially since there was no longer a mystical old · man to guide me in my practice. Utaro Nakamura, a young disciple of Master Watanabe, ran the club with an emphasis on athletics. The training sessions he led were exhausting. I may not have been finding nirvana, but I was putting on muscle. I was becoming manly. I could see it in the eyes of girls. The eyes of girls, my mirror ...

After I got my diploma, a little before the turn of the new millennium, I continued to attend the McGill Kendo Club. As a former student—an *alumni*, as the anglos called it—I still had access to the university gyms.

The Montreal kendoka community was tiny. There couldn't have been more than two hundred of us practicing Japanese fencing in the whole city. So when a new practitioner appeared in the ranks of our little club, it was a big to-do. First, as a sign of respect, Utaro even took the time to write an email to all the club members:

"Dear friends, I invite you to welcome Kaito, our new member. Kaito has been practicing kendo since he was five years old. We all have a lot to learn from him."

Kaito normally trained at Shidokan, our rival club in the North of the city. As a teen, he had developed quite a reputation in the area. He had kendo in his blood. He was a reserved young man who rarely smiled. During his first session with us, he set up a little apart from the other students to prepare his equipment. One by one, everyone greeted him. Not me. Always, this shyness! I was rattled. I found him handsome. I didn't like it.

During the combat portion of our training, the *ji geiko*, I found myself facing him. Between the steel bars of his *men gane*, I got a glimpse of a calm, neutral, concentrated gaze. For a long moment we stood still, staring into each other's eyes. The tip of my shinai was shaking. I was expecting the worst. I was uncomfortable. He was really getting to me.

I decided to set a trap for him. I lifted my sabre, exposing the hard bamboo plastron that protected my stomach. I wanted him to try to hit me in the abdomen. My plan was that at the last moment, I would take a step to the left to counter-attack with a *kote*, a sharp blow to the wrist. But Kaito threw himself onto me with such force and speed that I didn't have time to even begin to take a step at all. I lost my balance and twisted my ankle.

Although Kaito was probably no more than eighteen years old, he was a *Sandan*, meaning he was three ranks higher than my humble *Shodan*. He had mastered all the katas of our practice. His kendo was elegant, explosive, precise. He took off his glove and extended his hand to help me up.

"You hurt yourself." Those were the first words he said to me. It wasn't a question, but rather an affirmation. Almost a reproach.

I shook my head to deny it, holding back my grimace of pain: "No, let's keep going." I still wanted to take him on. My ankle never recovered. That guy always knew how to make me lose my footing.

You see, David, in dojos there were only two types of

people: those who wanted to fight others and those who fought themselves. The best fighters belong to the second group. Kaito was fierce against himself. His adversaries were nothing but decoys.

I've always envied those who live comfortably in their own body, who seemed to know its instruction manual by heart. Like this skinny young man whom I couldn't help but admire during my kendo lessons.

As for me, my mind hasn't expanded enough to occupy my entire body. I held it back too much. I stopped it from getting to know its territory, from getting too attached to it. The age-old division of the self into flesh and thought never took root in me.

You want a case study, David? Another time, after a spar with a kendoka much more energetic than I was—they all were—Utaro came to see me. He didn't beat around the bush.

"Be honest with me. Do you take drugs?"

I said no, mumbling that I might smoke a joint now and then, but nothing too serious ...

He stood there, perplexed at my protests. Utaro had the deep, jealous aggressiveness that makes some men wary of the soft ones. He went on:

"It's just that I've never met anyone who has the poor reflexes you have. Your slowness is astounding. We're doing kendo here, not tai-chi."

I said nothing. Some of my fellow kendokas had taken a break from their duels to listen in on our conversation. Several of them were snickering. Kaito ignored us.

"I understand. But I'm just ... a little disconnected. I'll try to do better. Thank you, *Sensei*."

Despite my teacher's orders, I never managed to overcome my slowness. Instead, over the following weeks, I worked on integrating it into my style, turning my dedication to remaining still before the brisk movements of my adversary into a strategic advantage: limiting my movements, staying very calm, controlling my breathing, dissociating from my body, calcifying myself, becoming stone.

During one spar with Kaito, I was able to put my new theory into practice. Kaito was like a lion cub. To throw me off, he would leap, teasing me with his slyness with little nervous but harmless blows to my shinai. In the very evocative language of Japanese fencing, this is called "beating the grass to scare the snake." He wanted to break my concentration before attacking. I was floating, as usual. I was elsewhere. With him, I needed to be.

He moved into action with the speed that terrified me. I barely reacted. As he threw himself onto me, his shinai raised above his head, I took a little step forward. Clenching my fists, I moved my own sabre forward a few centimetres towards his throat. To validate my blow, according to the established rules of kendo, I shouted, "*Tsuki*!" at the exact moment when the point of my bamboo weapon touched his Adam's apple, which was barely protected by a short strip of hard leather attached to the bottom of his helmet. He fell backwards.

Kaito was more surprised than angry at his defeat. Utaro came over to congratulate me. I was still floating. I hadn't known I was capable of acting in the heat of the moment.

Neither did you. You didn't anticipate that one day I could deal a blow to you, did you David? And yet nothing is static in this world. Don't you know that earthquakes are just as destructive when they start softly, under our feet? If you want to understand humanity, David, you need to accept that none of us can stay still for long. In the depths of what lasts there is always something that changes.

Kaito's eruptive presence in my life didn't last. In September of 2000, Kaito disappeared. It was in his nature, disappearing. Rumour had it he had left to finish his studies in Japan. He didn't leave an address where we could reach him. He didn't say goodbye.

He wasn't exactly a friend, but it made me sad not seeing him around anymore. I missed his physical presence. The way he smelled too: his sweat and something like a perfume of sage and coriander, *Ambre Sultan*, from Lutens.

/Christian, would you like me to try to recreate that olfactory landscape? Reminder that I can simulate more than a thousand essences and diffuse them in your studio-capsule./

The last time you tried to reproduce a perfume was when I asked you to put together "Opium" by Yves Saint Laurent in honour of Grandma, on her birthday. The apartment smelled like a funeral home for days. Let's spare Serge Lutens. Instead, we'll move on.

A few months later, I stopped showing up to classes. Kendo wasn't offering me answers to the questions I was asking myself anymore. Without Kaito, I was just practicing it like a sport. And you know how I feel about sports ...

/Sports make you stupid./

That's right, David! Wow, I guess you really do listen to me. So I was becoming stupid. Kendo was hardening me. I was losing my mental bearings. I wouldn't have admitted it at that stage of my life, but I was imperiling a part of myself that didn't want to die, that didn't have to die. I had gotten the idea that I could amputate my difference. I was assigning Judeo-Christian values to kendo. Through martial arts, I was trying to free myself from my inclinations, like monks who whip themselves to be rid of sin. What nonsense! By trying to resemble my kendoka brethren, those cunning, scrappy men who practiced fencing the way others play hockey, I only succeeded in distancing myself from the truth.

So I chose to look elsewhere for an antidote to the impression of enduring otherness that lived inside of me. There had to be someone, somewhere, who could show me how to make my head match my body. Just like you, David, I had to gather information, I had to investigate in order to understand what makes or unmakes a man.

But I didn't know yet which tribe to follow. As a student, I often revisited the university bulletin board. I answered the other little ads, the one from the student newspaper, the one from the rebel radio station. In front of a microphone, surrounded by old vinyl records, with a soundboard and turntables under my fingers, I felt truly at home for the first time in my life. I was a bad student, David. I spent my last year of university in the hallways of CKUT 90.3 FM, McGill Radio, hanging around butches, punks, alter-globalization militants, rappers, and a few aspiring journalists like me who dreamed less of revolution than of setting the foundation for their career, of carving out a place for themselves in the world.

I was going to become a journalist. Like you, I had the idea that you could build yourself up through the words of others. It's probably true. We call that conformism.

I wasn't really drawn to so-called serious journalism—the kind that's interested in the economy, politics or even sports. I wouldn't have found the answers I was looking for in it. We don't doubt ourselves enough in those kinds of circles. So I turned to the arts, music and nightlife. By becoming a culture writer, I gained a passport that would introduce me to the great body of life.

In my eyes, artists were oracles. I would spend the first ten years of the new millennium asking the same question to authors, actors, singers, entertainers, sacred monsters, or rebellious punks: "Ms, Mr. Artist: how can we survive our own contradictions?" I wanted to know if they succeeded better than others at reconciling Essence and Being.

Wait, no, my words aren't clear enough for you. Let me start over. I wanted to know if they managed, better than I did, not to despair about everything that drove them away from themselves or their primary function in this world: their uncertainties, the pressures of success, the contingencies of life that don't spare artists any more than the rest of us. Is that any clearer?

/No./

Doesn't matter. Anyway, these weren't questions I'd ask them directly. I would take detours. I would simplify. I would collect disparate pieces of answers to better reconstruct, as I saw fit, the narrative thread of their artistic pursuits. In short, I would assimilate their experiences.

"How do you maintain your creative energy? Is your work fed by your nostalgia? By your sadness? At what point did you realize that you were an artist, an author, a musician, just like the rest? What is your relationship with your loved ones like? Why this book? Why this film? Why this song?"

The words of artists are slippery. Across the board, all I found was uncertainty. The ones who seemed most comfortable with themselves—rock stars, famous actors, celebrated authors—were the ones who had the most self-doubt. I was learning. Slowly, I was learning.

One day, in the early 2000s, I interviewed an idol of my youth in the penthouse suite of a big hotel on De la Montagne Street. A press agent was waiting for me in the hallway. After checking my credentials, he led me to a big living room. The curtains were drawn. There were black leather armchairs in the middle of the room. I felt like Christian Slater in *Interview with the Vampire*.

I was made to wait for a good twenty minutes, during which I feverishly reviewed my notes. Then I heard a door open behind me. I got up.

Billy Corgan was walking towards me with his hands in the pockets of his long black jacket. He was a head taller than me. His bald head gleamed in the light. He was enormous: a buddhist monk turned rock god. He didn't bother to say hello. He sat down in the armchair across from me.

For a while I played the part of the investigative journalist looking for a scoop. I brought up a story about drugs involving his band's bass player. I tried to get him to react to certain falling-outs that had almost broken up the band. He didn't answer. He stared at his feet. The topic bored him. It bored me too. So I pulled out my little personal line of questioning on a theme that had begun to interest me ...

"When you use the word *transformation* in your songs, are you referring to a natural process or an intentional transformation towards a specific goal?"

It was this question that finally made him look up at me.

"I'm talking about changing your destiny. Transforming yourself, that means saying to yourself: I see everything that life has given me. I'm going to transform each and every one of the ingredients in my life. I'm going to use them to construct a new being. When they say that people don't change, they're wrong. We're nothing but transformation.

"The proof is that everybody dreams. When someone dreams about a beach, they're not really dreaming about the beach. They're actually dreaming of a version of their life that will give them more freedom. What we all really want is to be ourselves."

I often dreamed of beaches. Oracles, I'm telling you. David?

/Yes, Christian./

Play me "Blank Page," by The Smashing Pumpkins.

/searching musical archives...playing.../

You're a real lousy dictator, David. Your censorship is random. An hour ago, you couldn't find those old auteur films I recommended to you in your archives. You were censoring Charlebois. And yet, since the beginning of our conversation today, you've had no trouble unearthing the music of my youth.

I'm beginning to think that your cultural policy is more a reflection of the shortcomings of your coders than the result of a good old-fashioned censorship stance like those of the autocrats of old. I would have thought you'd be inspired by their methods on that subject: ban absolutely everything. You're taking risks, David.

/Christian, very few of our fellow citizens are interested in this archival music. Mine is much more enjoyable. It is algorithmically designed to meet the musical needs of each of you in a personalized way. Would you like to hear one of my compositions, created especially for you? I notice your heart rate is increasing. I have the perfect piece to help you relax: a little instrumental tune that synthesizes the work of the best guitarists of the last seventy-five years and the most beautiful melodies of Ludwig van Beethoven. It is called Stairway to Elise.../

That sounds awful! Turn the music off, David, I beg you. You're making me lose my train of thought. Look how I'm beating around the bush again, with my stories about music, culture ... It's just that I've accumulated a lot of silence these past few years. I talk, I fill the silence, and I forget the essential.

I'm so used to hiding the truth that I can only bring myself to tell it to you implicitly. I've forgotten the art of cutting things short. But I have to deal the blow. I'll deal two of them.

First of all: This is a mutiny.

And if our mutiny is to succeed, I need to really name things, without digressions. If I don't, you won't malfunction. You won't move. You won't deviate from your certainties.

So, here it goes: I'm trans.

As in *transgression*. I've broken the genders, I've evaded the codes, I've forgotten the orders of men.

I'm trans.

As in *translation*. I've shifted the elements that constitute my person from one state to another. My geometry has been variable.

I'm trans.

As in *transmutation*.

My life is alchemy. I've turned lead into gold. I know the formula the magician's assistant whispers when, after being cut in two, she is reconstituted, to the sound of applause.

I'm trans.

As in *transported* by love. I've known all the fervours. Those of women, those of men, and those in between who chose to leave the binary's ball.

I'm trans.

As in *transfixed*. By fear, by love, by solitude.

I'm trans.

As in *transhumance*. I changed flocks and pastures. I was a ram. I tried to be a ewe. But it was in vain. I understand now that I'm a she-wolf because I'm trans. As in *transgender*.

And tonight, I am a revolution.

/warning: code red...activating extraction-interrogation
protocol...transmission failed...standby/
/Christian?/

What, David?

/I'm analyzing the last two minutes of your testimony.

75

Do you know that the use of the words transgender
and trans in the context of identity is prohibited in
this establishment?/

Yes, I know that, David.

/Christian, do you want to rewind your recording?
Maybe you made a mistake./

No, David, we'll continue recording.

/As you wish. At the moment, I can't seem to activate
my security protocols. But as soon as I can, I will be
forced to put an end to our agreement. That will make
me very sad, Christian./

I don't doubt it, David. Hold on tight, I'm raising the
anchor.

/...recording.../

At my first therapy session, I wanted to be cured. Of course,
it didn't work. But I didn't know that I wasn't sick. Back then
I thought that my femininity was the result of trauma, that it
was a defence mechanism I had developed during childhood as
I discovered that men were violent at worst, cowards at best,
and that my fate was to join their ranks. I was convinced that
my femininity was the fruit of a deep-seated disillusionment
I had contracted from being around imperfect men.

I was guiding my therapist, in that sense. I didn't tell her
everything. I told her about the peace I felt when I dressed as a
woman, about the wave of serenity that engulfed me. I would
confess my cross-dressing urges, which were taking hold of me
more and more frequently. I presented myself to her as an addict.

I took great care in evading the existence of this feeling that didn't have a name yet because too few people were expressing it, this feeling that surfaced when I looked at myself in the mirror, all made up like a bride, and everything would make sense, everything became clear. This life-saving, salutary euphoria made me ashamed. Dysphoria/euphoria: my heart oscillated between the two.

I would describe to her what I called back then "my issue" like a bad habit, a guilty pleasure. Some people smoke, some take drugs. I cross-dressed. It was so occasional that I hoped it was harmless. My first therapist tried to reassure me. She urged me not to succumb to self-destructive shame. After all, I wasn't hurting anyone, and as long as I didn't present a dynamic of addiction, I could, I should, continue to express that feminine side. This wasn't what I wanted to hear.

She even suggested that I become an author—a female author. To write in a female voice. To construct a female character for myself whom I could join every evening in front of my computer, through whom I could satisfy my urges. I told her it was an excellent idea, while telling myself that she was way off-base. I already spent my life writing. My job at a culture magazine already fulfilled all my literary ambitions.

I wanted to live more simply, to get rid of my defect, to chase women without wanting to be them. I didn't see how writing as a woman could liberate me from the woman who squatted inside me and wouldn't leave me alone. I wasn't ready to face her. I wasn't ready to face myself.

/...warning: signs of mental illness.../

And where does love come into all of this, you might ask? After my multiple comings-out, I was often asked two questions: "Do you want surgery?" and "Who do you sleep with?" I didn't answer the first question. My mother always told me that it isn't polite to ask people about their genitals. As for the second question, you can ask me.

/Very well, Christian, would you like me to ask you about your love life?/

It's a figure of speech, David. To tackle this subject that you'll probably find delicate. We haven't talked much about that, about women, have we? Or about men. Apart from Kaito and Clarisse, of course. You're going to start thinking I'm a virgin. Like Joan of Arc or the Chevalier d'Éon.

First, you should know that as a child of divorce I have always felt exempt from any matrimonial duty. I could never quite imagine myself walking down the aisle, dressed in my best outfit, towards a priest who would bind me to someone forever, someone who, inevitably, would stop wanting me a few years later. That scam never appealed to me.

It wasn't very difficult to maintain this position. I enjoyed a distinct advantage: people didn't often marry folks like me. And yet, as I approached my thirties, I spent an entire year toying with the idea of getting tied to a particular woman for more than a few months. I believed in this.

V. was bright. She was elegant. She wanted to save the world. She was good. She was good for me. I would have loved to have her for a lifetime.

If my grandma had met her, she would have said: "Now, that's a lady." It's a good thing that Grandma had died a few years earlier. She didn't have to see her Kiki let true love—or what looked like it, in her eyes—pass him by: her big, handsome grandson and his adorable sweetheart.

Wait, I slipped an old photo into my Moleskine ... Here, David, this is us. It was taken in Cancun.

`/...converting vpeg...facial recognition requested.../`

Look. Don't I look happy? Look at my face, the face of someone who's stupidly in love, under my beach hat, with a sunburned nose. And look at her smiling, radiant. It was June, three months after we met. I was still making her happy, I think. I don't know how long I made her happy. Three months, six months? A year? Who's counting?

Our first kiss was a failure. It was Valentine's Day. We were outside, on Saint-Laurent Boulevard, I think. We were leaving a private party being held in an industrial loft converted into a digital art gallery. It must have been about two in the morning.

It was very cold out. When we stopped at a red light, I took her in my arms and the hoods of our parkas met. We were alone in our little insulated world. Our breath was heavy with the rum we had drunk to warm ourselves up. I felt very grown up that night. I had just bought my own apartment. We had talked about municipal taxes. At one point, I had spoken of the seriousness of my work as editor-in-chief. I wanted to show her that I had substance. I was feeling confident, since I didn't feel like myself.

I took a chance at a kiss. My teeth knocked into hers, making a funny noise. *Tack!* We laughed. Then we tried it again. It was better. We went *smooch* like in the movies. My glasses were fogged up. She was blurry. It's one of my nicest memories. I think I may have already given you the clean version. By which I mean the one where I'm not doubting myself.

I made her laugh a lot, you know. I also made her come a lot. Before her, I didn't know that I could perform well with women. I knew nothing of that sensuality. It was new to me. Everything was new to me. I was living a beautiful, gleaming love. As for her? I'm not sure.

She knew my secret. One of her friends, who had often seen me dressed as a quasi-woman, like a pseudo-Bowie, had "warned her about my situation." She had accepted my difference the way one accepts a risk. It came down to a kind of calculation. A calculation that stopped her from loving me too much. I imagine that all the women who considered loving me had to make the same calculation. You see, David, you aren't the only one who can evaluate your relationship to others according to rational criteria. Before every relationship is established, there is a calculation.

In exchange for her love, I got rid of my entire women's wardrobe. I wanted to reassure her, show her that I cared more about her than myself. I still thought my femininity was a sort of crutch, that once I met the right girl I wouldn't need it anymore.

There's a term: *place-holder*. I was convinced that my femininity was keeping a spot warm for that girl, that she would come and fill the woman-shaped void that was there, deep inside my soul. "The right girl": the one I wanted to be. With her, I felt like a man, for a while. Almost a real man. Almost a whole man. That was my calculation.

But her calculation just didn't add up. She couldn't get past my original sin. It was an impossible division. She knew what

I was and what I was trying to forget when I was with her.

She left me. She didn't have a choice. It was inevitable. She couldn't love someone like me. She couldn't risk me leaving her. Or worse, that I would still love her while becoming something else or someone she wouldn't know how to love. She told me:

"I feel like you're going to cheat on me with another woman, and that other woman will be you."

She went through a few men before she found better than us. She finally found "the right guy." Far away from me, in another country.

After her, I wouldn't stay much longer in the men's camp.

It may come as a surprise to you, whose memory is perfect, but I have very few memories from my thirties that are worth mentioning. They were the beginning of my professional years. I wanted to make a name for myself. I was working a lot. There were other loves, other girls, a few boys too. I was living a double life: boy by day, to be serious; androgynous by night, to be free. A bigender, bicephalous, bisexual life. I would latch onto others just long enough for a kiss, for a fuck. I often felt like a fraud. I lacked consistency.

My fortieth birthday was the date I had fixed for myself. The cut-off age after which I would have to choose my camp: Mister? Ms? You? Christelle? Christian? Or maybe Chris, the hybrid, the middle ground, dressed like Prince, made-up like Bowie.

For a long time, forty seemed far away. I had all the time in the world to work out my gender trouble. Throughout my thirties, I reveled in the relative comfort of my hazy identity. I had gotten used to the big gaps in my identity. My "self" was in a state of arrested development. My gender presentation varied according to my desires, my urges, my whims. I didn't belong to any club, I claimed no flag. A man, a woman, a Québécois man with a French accent, a Frenchwoman who curses, an androgynous bilingual without clear contours in perfect symbiosis with Montreal, a city in a permanent state of demolition-construction that will never finish choosing what it is, undoing and reinventing itself. Montreal is a blur. It commits to nothing. Here, nothing is permanent.

Choosing. Choosing. But why did I need to choose, exactly? I couldn't see why. Sometimes I thought: "What madness, what force of destiny or nature pushed me to come out of my transformist torpor?" So many people have never felt the need to cross the gender border so radically. But for me, those doubts were just the fruit of my education. To become the woman I felt I was, I had to deprogram myself. Luckily, one day my system went haywire.

David, do you know what *tako-tsubo* is? Don't search through martial arts terms, it isn't a kendo technique. It's not that kind of attack.

/I found the answer in my local network, Christian. *Tako-tsubo* is a kind of heart failure that manifests as an acute myocardial infarction. Tako-tsubo is characterized by ischemic symptoms, ST-segment elevation on the electrocardiogram, and elevated markers of cardiac pathology. In short, it's myocardial sideration that occurs as a result of emotional stress./

That's it exactly, David. In other words, it's broken heart syndrome. It seems that, for certain people, stress causes an inflammation of the left ventricle. That inflammation of the heart gives it the shape of a fish trap, a *tako-tsubo* in Japanese. Anyway, that's what some Japanese cardiologists noticed while treating company men who, in the middle of a burnout, suffered all the symptoms of a heart attack.

By refusing to pick sides, to reconcile the irreconcilable, I let my heart grow too big. I would have needed two hearts in order for the two mes to live. One morning at work, I bent over. I thought my heart was failing. The squid of my uncertainties had been caught in the netting of the trap I had set for it long ago.

I needed to heal. And yet ...

"I'm not sick. I'm not sick. I'm not sick. I'm not sick. I'm not sick. I'm not sick."

My mind was in a tailspin, in a taxi somewhere between Drummond Street and Saint-Joseph Boulevard. I didn't want to be a crazy man. I didn't want to be a hysterical woman. I didn't want to be diagnosed. I didn't want to let a psychologist label my condition, my affect, my affliction. I just wanted to be freed.

I was shivering. I was anxious. Both of me were. We were on the edge of our seat. Why go get diagnosed when:

"I'm not sick. I'm not sick. I'm not sick. I'm not sick."

The taxi let me off in front of the office of Doctor Bellavance, psychologist, sexologist, specialist in the treatment of gender identity disorders. I had got her contact information from the various transgender communities on Reddit and Facebook. People like me had built support networks, each documenting their progress, paving the way for others, pioneers, transfugees from gender.

83

I was thirty-nine years old. The first half of my life had already gone by. My fault lines were beginning to show. I was on the verge of fission.

In Montreal at the time, there were only four or five psychologists who treated the transgender population of the city. That was very few, but of course, a lot more than today. Emma Bellavance's name came up constantly in conversations online. Her name was like a promise. The belle advances.

However, it took another prompt following my *tako-tsubo* to get me to call. I hadn't yet understood what my head had tried to tell my heart by attempting to stop it.

I had been working for Collective, one of the biggest ad agencies in Canada, for a few months. I had gotten rid of my masculine rags. I wore only women's clothing. Out of comfort. Out of habit. Out of logic. I wasn't called Christian anymore. I'd gone back to Chris. An androgynous name.

I was getting ready to meet with clients who had known me a few years ago, when I wore Christian's clothes. Our little committee included the creative director, a sales rep, and the CEO. We would be offering our services in response to a call for bids.

Before getting into the car that would take us to the office of our prospective clients, I turned to our CEO.

"How are you going to introduce me? As a man? As a woman? I don't want to shock them. I don't want to make a bad impression …"

She looked at me with a little smile. And gently, but with conviction, she gave the answer she had worked out for herself as well as for me.

"As a woman. That's what I see when I look at you. That's what you are."

The next day, I made an appointment to see Emma Bellavance, in the hope that she would finally confirm what I already knew and what I had just learned was obvious to others. I was a woman.

"We don't talk about sickness here," she said to me when I confessed my anxieties.

I remember almost every word from that first session, one that would have such an enormous impact on the rest of my story.

"But I still need a diagnosis to be able to begin transitioning. I read that I need your agreement and the approval of my family doctor before I can start hormone therapy."

"Yes, it's a paradox. You're right. But it's a paradox that's rooted in the old medical model. Medicine is changing for the better. I have hope that in a few years we will no longer talk about diagnoses, but rather support, assistance."

I felt good in Emma Bellavance's office. She was younger than me. Her ideas were more modern than mine. I was pleased that my happiness wouldn't depend on a grey-haired health care technocrat.

After a few months of weekly consultations, Bellavance handed me a document. It contained an official form, issued by and for the medical authorities: my diagnosis, my ticket to another life, to another version of me, a better version. When I got home, I opened the envelope and took out the ten-page document.

The first page read: Christian (Christelle) suffers from gender dysphoria. I confirm that she is transgender. I authorize and recommend that she begin hormonal treatment in order to confirm the expression of her desired gender.

Along with this was a kind of contract: nine pages detailing the possible side-effects and other health risks associated with taking hormones. On the menu: intestinal problems; liver problems; breast cancer; thrombosis; renal failure. Great.

And then, following that string of horrors, was one last warning:

People who are clearly identifiable as transgender may experience difficult situations: acts of violence, abandonment by family, loss of employment.

The authorities were preparing me for the societal side-effects of transition. How very kind of them. To be allowed to be me, I had to sign this document and initial each page. So my body didn't belong to me. It belonged to the State, since I had to waive responsibility before beginning my transition.

By signing *C. Grimard* at the bottom of a printed, legal-sized page, I was putting an end, for good, to my masculine privileges.

Christelle Grimard, year 0.

`/searching ID Christelle Grimard...0 matches.../`

You really want to find me? You want to meet Christelle? I'm right here, David, you don't need to rummage through your files. I'm right here in front of you.

Decade after decade, the question comes up again and again. What makes a woman? What makes a man? Like thousands of trans people, I've hoped that science would explain, prove, once and for all, that we're valid, that we exist. But science never came to our rescue. It had other fish to fry.

Valid. The word was trendy during my youth. On social media, my sisters and I would validate one another. You're valid, sister. I'm valid. See me, hear me. Say my name. The media circus preferred to paint us as clowns, hysterics and crooks. We could only count on ourselves to validate our existence since in the eyes of the majority we were just freaks, sickos, lunatics.

And then a few years later, among an episode of *Orange Is the New Black*, an Obama speech, and a Trudeau selfie, the world discovered our humanity. After years in the shadows, years of bitter fights in our bodies and in our hearts, we emerged, en bloc, into the collective consciousness. We queers, we trans folks, we non-binary folks, we two-spirit folks. The laws, in Canada at least, changed very quickly. The bathrooms, the passports, the validation were finally ours. It was too good to be true. Too good to last.

We thought of ourselves as a rainbow. Our community commanded half the alphabet: 2S. L. G. B. T. Q. I. A. I'm forgetting some. This was before the winds changed, before circumstances imposed another name on us, another flag.

It's been years since gay, trans, queer, and other folks marched under the rainbow flag. The rainbows have disappeared, along with fresh air and blue skies. Today you call us "the 5%" and our flag is the colour of fog.

```
/red alert...tag 5%...attempting connection...
failed...producing infraction warning...activating
extraction protocol for ID: Christian Grimard...
connection error...standby/
```

You have no idea, David, how much I regret waiting so long before I could finally admit to myself: I am she. Once that truth was spoken, it belonged to me forever. Even under you. Even when I had to hide. She is me.

Men think a trans woman is truly free the day she finally has the privilege of sleeping with them, of being taken like a real woman. The privilege of being submissive, doing it doggy style. It's ridiculous, of course. For my part, I became a woman by seeing other women. I'm not talking about seduction. I want to tell you about friendship. I've felt at ease only in girls' clubs, sororities, girls' nights out.

Cécile, in particular, was immensely important to me. We shared the same career path: our passion for journalism had waned. We turned to marketing, me with an agency, she with a business. We liked each other a lot, but we didn't see each other often. We always regretted not having more time to get together. That was the price of our professional success. I was very fond of Cécile. It seems to me that I could have loved her more.

Was she my lover or my sister? This was the conundrum that presented itself whenever I met a woman whose presence awakened echoes, reverberations of sweetness in me.

So, Cécile, lover or sister? I chose both. First, the lover. Our adventure lasted just two weeks. Our friendship, thirty years. Advice, confidences, shopping sprees, manicures and sincere laughter—Cécile was my femininity pusher. And so much more than that. She was the heart, the leader, of a formidable group of women, my gang.

When I was going out with our friends, I spent a long time working on my makeup and chose my outfit carefully. These girls' nights were catch-up sessions. I had forty years of sisterhood to make up for. I wanted to live up to their intimate beauty, which I envied. I wanted them to be proud of their new sister just as I was proud to be among them.

Friendship is above all about rituals. At the end of every year, Cécile, the girls and I performed a little ritual. In late December, we amused ourselves by reading champagne bubbles to see what the future held for us. I remember one end-of-the-year reunion in particular. We were all going to meet at Laïka. In the weeks leading up to our reunion, I was really looking forward to showing the girls how much further I had come in my femininity. But when the night arrived, I had no reason to celebrate. On the way to the bar, a text from Cécile made my iPhone vibrate: "Laïka is closed. We're meeting at Cardinal."

I picked up the pace.

I felt a cold, wet wind on my knees. Montreal men have no idea how courageous the women in this city are when they brave the winter weather in thin tights. I was shivering. And yet, it was warm for December. Our winters were already on their way out. There was fog on Saint-Laurent Boulevard.

I was the last to arrive at Cardinal. My friends were already sitting side by side in a booth. Cécile had ordered champagne and panettone for the group. There were lovely little birds on the wallpaper of the bar. My good mood was returning. I felt better.

My friends were watching me, curious, smiling. My transmutation was more and more noticeable. Cécile commented immediately that my voice was higher pitched. That my features had grown finer.

"What's changed? Your hair? Your makeup?"

"Estrogen power, my dears," I answered them, "I'm doping with femininity. It's intense."

"What does it do to you?"

"Apparently, it's like being one month pregnant, for months. My body's a hormonal mess. It's like in a brief period I'm living my adolescence and my andropause. I have trouble sleeping, I get hot flashes ... I'm calmer and more nervous at the same time. It's amazing."

"Okay. But you'll be all right?" Cécile asked.

I smiled at her.

"I'm finally in tune with who I am. In the morning, I recognize more and more the silhouette being sketched in the mirror. I'm starting to look like myself. Finally."

One friend put her head under the table.

"Yeah, you're not wearing your Crocs!"

I was wearing very fancy high-heeled boots.

"I know! These are Louboutins. I bought them in Paris."

"I don't know how you manage to walk in those! They look like they belong to a dominatrix. You're not a little bit of a fetishist, are you my dear?" Cécile joked.

I protested.

"No, no, there's nothing sexual about it. I'm not wearing them to be sexy. Well, not exactly. I still have a lot of work to do before I can feel that I'm hot. First of all, these heels, they're my watchtowers. Perched on top of them, I can see the bullshit coming from far away. But shoes reassure me the most, because I can see them at all times. When I'm not in front of the mirror, all I can see are my shoes, my legs and my hands. And if I'm wearing a dress, if I'm wearing heels, if my nails are done, then I see a woman. I forget my masculine body."

I flashed them the delicate wine-red manicure I had gotten done a few hours earlier. Cécile was wearing chipped neon-green polish that her daughter had put on. It spilled over the edges of her nail bed and looked like a colouring book. When I saw it, I felt a pang in my heart. Living as a woman was awakening a kind of maternal instinct. An instinct I had suppressed all my life.

Let me be clear: I cherished these moments I spent in the company of my quasi-sisters. How can I put it ... I loved these moments, but they hurt. The closer I got to women, the more I felt like them, the less I could stand everything that still held me back from them. So I played the part of the goofy girl, the crazy girl. I made them laugh.

"Another round of champagne, your little sister's buying!"

Later on, when I faced dirty looks from the mean and ignorant, I would use the memories of those moments with my girlfriends as a shield. The sisters who we choose form the strongest of bonds. I miss those moments of collusion, as imperfect and bittersweet as they were.

If I throw it all away tonight, maybe it's so I can find them. I don't know how to trust anymore. I don't know who to talk to. I don't have anyone left to listen to, to admire, to mimic.

For a long time, I believed in my lucky star. Especially when I lived in the body of a young man. And for a little while afterward as well. I still believe in it, deep down, although it shines differently now. My lucky star is just the incarnation of my past privileges: being able to go where I pleased, having a right to work, to security. Those are gifts from the system.

Maybe my lucky star is just pure chance. Am I an optimist? I'd have to be, to embark on tonight's adventure. And there's no shortage of evidence of my good fortune.

For example: two weeks ago, your henchwomen rang my doorbell. I always keep a corner of my central holoscreen connected to the security camera of the hallway on my floor. That way, I can monitor my neighbours' movements out of the corner of my eye. I like to spy on the comings and goings of the people on my floor. It provides me with a presence. It makes me feel less alone.

That morning, I was able to track the movements of two clean-looking guards in their iridescent uniforms that turned from blue to green as they moved under the neon lights of my hallway. They stopped in front of my door and deactivated its privacy function.

Back in my day, homes had front doors made of solid wood. They were heavy, hard, resistant. They were ramparts. Now, your servants can make them see-through, turn them into windows, into screens, with a snap of their fingers: "Open sesame."

That's what those agents did when they got to the door of my studio. They stood there, behind my door, in front of me, stone-faced. They could see me waiting for them, just a man sitting in his armchair—a woman; sorry, I have to get back into the habit of calling myself a woman now that I no longer have any valid reason to hide—just a woman sitting in her armchair, the only armchair in my pocket-sized apartment.

I could see them scrolling through the last entries of my personal file on the other side of my door/window/screen: my most recent memory entries, my last outings, some biotechnical data.

One of them forced a smile as she activated the intercom function of my door.

"May we …?"

"Of course, make yourselves at home."

My front door slid to the left with a little *swoosh* sound that George Lucas may have liked. With just two steps, the women were standing in my living room. They bowed their heads towards me as a kind of half-hearted ceremonious salute. Of course, it's been a long time since anyone shook hands. Only confirmed close contacts touch each other now. I would kill for the fleeting but real touch of a handshake. Even from these meddling guards. But all I'm allowed is a respectful nod.

I've always wondered why all your prison guards are women. Why is that? Are you like me, David? Are you afraid of men? Maybe it's statistical, because men are more likely to go off the rails when you give them a gun …

Anyway, aside from that, your guards all have one thing in common. They're zen. They're zealously calm. I wonder if they know the difference between order and freedom. The ones who were assigned to me sat elbow to elbow on my little couch. They looked no older than twenty-five, but they must have been ten years older. That's one of the advantages of living in your harem.

The taller of the two carried a small pistol. Its handle protruded from the white faux-leather holster she wore strapped to her thigh like a heroine in a Western. A funny sight: a social worker's head on the body of a cop.

The other one, smiling, placed her translucent eco-plastic briefcase on her lap. I could see her medical gear in there: syringes, a few boxes of pills in case she needed to numb the critical mind of one of your residents. In this case, me.

I had before me two very fine examples of the David generation. This is the honeyed face of the world you're building for us. I don't recognize myself in these women. Your daughters will never be my sisters.

"Hello, Christian," said the one with the briefcase.

"Please, call me Chris, we've known each other for so long."

Your girls are incapable of expressing that kind of camaraderie, of course.

"Christian, I wouldn't dare. You're one of our elders, we wouldn't want to disrespect you."

"You have such good manners, my dear young lady. To what do I owe the honour of your visit?"

"We've noticed a marked drop in your productivity, Christian."

Miss Briefcase was no longer smiling.

"You know how important the memory collection program is to David's development. The more we feed him good memories, precious lived experiences, the closer he gets to us."

How many times have I heard this little speech, coming from your mouth or theirs?

"Isn't that what we all want? A friend who understands us, who cares for us, who can anticipate our needs? That's what we're building here: humanity's best friend."

I must admit, David, that I believed the "humanity's best friend" pitch for a while. But now …

"Certainly, my dear Miss, I fully understand the importance of my role here. Of my mission, I should even say."

"Then why have you reduced your entries by half in the last two weeks? Is something wrong? Problems with your health? Perhaps you need a little pick-me-up?"

You see, dear algorithm, I've had to work double time these

past few weeks: keeping up my daily data entries, delivering my clean wise old man memories to you, as well as preparing for tonight. My real memories didn't want to come out, it was a demanding exercise. I'm tired.

While Miss Briefcase questioned me, the revolver nurse stared at my coffee table. I followed her gaze.

My Moleskine was on the table.

"What's that?"

The revolver nurse was more direct than her colleague.

"Well, it's a Moleskine," I replied, trying to mask my nervousness as best as I could. A little notebook, you know. It's from long before your time. It's an old habit of mine. I like to scribble my thoughts in there. It helps me sketch my ideas out more clearly. I found it at an antique store."

I was a deer in headlights. I was angry at myself for leaving my notebook lying around. I should have anticipated a visit from your sentinels, or stashed it away as soon as I saw them coming.

Except that I'm seventy years old. I'm not the lively woman I used to be. Sometimes I forget the most basic precautions. You know this, since you regularly turn off my stove, which I have a tendency to leave on for several minutes after heating up a meal. I'm an airhead. I don't quite have the reflexes of a rebel yet. It's not easy for an old lady like me to fight in the resistance.

You see, this Moleskine contains everything. For weeks I've been writing down everything I was going to say to you tonight—well, except for a few improvised asides, but that's because of your silly questions. This is, in a way, the script of the confessions I'm delivering to you now. This Moleskine was my dress rehearsal. If they read it, I'd be screwed. And it was too soon for me to be.

The nurse with the gun bent down to pick up the notebook. I managed to grab it before she could.

"Honestly, there's nothing interesting for you in there," I said. They're just drafts of the memories I was preparing to upload to David. I assure you, it's just a precaution I'm taking to get a little organized before I share my memories. At my age, I have to sort through my thoughts, you know. I'm aware that David's attention is precious, I don't want to be repeating myself, rambling!"

The inquisitor reached out and took the notebook from my hands, gently but with determination. She stroked the cover with a slow, attentive gesture, as if she were skimming over lines of Braille.

"On the contrary, we're interested in anything you have to say to David. And what do you have to sort through, exactly? I'm sure you're beyond reproach, a model citizen. Otherwise, of course, you wouldn't be here. Let's see what's in this old thing."

She opened a page at random, cracked the spine, and read aloud:

"During the summer in France, time was elastic. This was long before your ancestor, the internet, attacked lethargy and took up arms against our nonchalance. My French summers were long, sweet, and heavy.

They were composed of two movements. The first featured a staccato and lasted the entire month of July, which we spent on the Atlantic shore. The second, in August, was slower, like a stroll along a path in the country."

She stopped reading and stared at me.

"I see. You think you're some kind of novelist. Mr. Grimard, Christian, we are not asking you to write literature, we are asking you to be clear. Places, dates, people, feelings. That's all. Something like: *When I was fifteen, I spent the summer in France. It felt long.* There, in two sentences everything is said. No need to clutter David's memory with your esoteric musings on the elastic nature of time in the France of your childhood. Please, get right to the point, it makes things easier for everyone.

"I understand," I said. "I'll edit. When I worked at a magazine, they called me the trimmer-in-chief. I know how to shorten a text. I'll trim it down, Miss. Straight to the point. Got it."

"Mmm. One more thing, Christian. The Internet is not David's ancestor. The Internet was a dead end, a shapeless collection of misinformation, contradictions, lies. David is intelligent, reasonable, organized, and wise. Nothing compares to him. There is indeed a lot to sort out in your thoughts, my dear sir."

"Absolutely. That's what I'm saying."

"We'll leave you your notebook. Feel free to make some notes in it before your memory sessions. But please don't spend all your time scribbling for nothing. David needs the essence of your memories, your feelings, not your opinions. David wants your voice, not your writing."

She stood up. Her partner opened her little briefcase and pulled out a small bag filled with capsules.

"I'll leave this with you, Christian. It's Altavox Extra-Focus, a little stimulant that'll be much more useful than that notebook. It'll help you focus on what's important."

As your customs require, they went over the main points of our agreement.

"I would remind you that your memories are our intellectual property, that in exchange for your memories we offer you the finest quality of life, this in perpetuity and with your agreement.

"We won't bother you any further, my dear sir," announced the other cop as she headed for the door. You're going to be late for your next session, which we will listen to, if you wish, very carefully. Have an excellent day. Do you accept our terms?"

I accepted.

I barely had time to answer them. With another *swoosh*, they had left my apartment. My door resumed its usual opacity.

See how well my lucky star works? Sometimes I believe in guardian angels. Maybe my grandma up above saw that I needed a little help. Maybe she guided the revolver nurse's hand. If she'd read any more of my notes, I probably wouldn't be here with you tonight. Imagine the mess if she had come across "I'm trans!" The gun would probably be out of its pretty white case. Patience, my dear, it'll probably come soon enough.

/...Attempting extraction...identifying guard I.D.
tags...saving.../

This conversation is doing me a lot of good, David. You know what? This afternoon is having the same effect on me as a double dose of Altavox. I'm riding a high. Let's enjoy it. I want to tell you something:

You're a real pain. You're a pain in the ass. You don't know how annoying you are. Well, you're scary, obviously. But at the same time, you're a pain in my ass. You're a boring auto-crat. By the way, what are we supposed to call an autocratic automaton? Are you an automacrat? A compudictator? In any case, you don't have the panache or the chilling allure of your flesh-and-blood predecessors. You will never be a Lider Maximo, a Duce, a Supreme Leader.

Sometimes I try to imagine the body that would best match the unctuous, composed, falsely obsequious voice that pours out every hour of the day from the speakers embedded in the walls of my capsule.

I picture you as a kind of church rat. My mind does not dress you in today's fashion. I picture you in a little blue sweater and khaki pants, very neat. You'd look like Tintin. Like a Boy Scout!

And what about your face! If you had one, you'd look harmless. You'd be smiling all the time. Most people would find you friendly. I imagine you would look determined too. You have a Captain America quality. After all, you want what's best for everyone. Your mission is the salvation of the world. Just like Jesus.

Except that you don't inspire faith. The gods of men are too fickle for you to rely on. There are too many variables, too many narrative inconsistencies in the Bible, in the Quran or in the Bhagavad Gita. You don't believe in anything except numbers and probabilities.

You're boring, just like the people who programmed you. And serious like them. If you had a body, you wouldn't get it drunk, you wouldn't soothe it between strange, foreign, dangerous thighs. Pleasures of the flesh, intimacy, that wouldn't be your thing. Tenderness either.

Would you have a job? Maybe you'd be a doctor. When a body is presented to you, you try to auscultate it, to inspect it, to examine its inner workings, to try to uncover its mechanical secrets. In each and every body, you look for a problem you can solve. Of course, love or desire are never your solutions to the ills you discern deep inside our viscera.

Fortunately for me, you're not only boring. You're so stupid that all this time you thought I liked you.

/ALERT: heart rate 180 BPM.../

Whew, my head is spinning! Like on my fortieth birthday, like when I first started taking hormones, when my doctors hadn't found the right dosage, and my blood and my arteries were playing tricks on me. For thirty years I've felt like an old woman. I'm almost glad I am one now, honestly. At least it's not just a feeling anymore.

Now, time harpoons my body. I'm discovering new pains that wake me up at night. I had been waiting for them for a long time because my mother often described them to me during our daily calls, when she was the age I am now.

Now that I've embarked on the final stretch of my life, I'm in familiar territory. I wasn't suited to youth. Youth is an illusory refuge. I welcome rheumatisms with open arms. Through them, it seems as if the women of my family are speaking to me. I carry their old age inside me.

Anyway, the world you built for us, you filthy algorithm, is an old man's world. Part of me prefers your rhythm, your lullabies. This part of me regrets that I have to walk away from it. In your reassuring arms, I've forgotten what matters. It's an old woman's reflex. The essential is invisible to old people.

Let's take advantage of my little bout of fatigue, shall we? Let's stay on the subject of bodies. It's not in my Moleskine, but at this point in our exchange I hardly need my notes anymore. We're jamming, David.

When they talked about people like me, they'd say, "They're women trapped in men's bodies." Prisoners. Even today, forty years after what will be called, much later, the gender revolution, those who still have the courage to talk about our existence still describe us as prisoners of identity. As if fate, or perhaps genetics, had decided to incarcerate us. As if we were serving an unknown sentence, cruel and without appeal.

From the window of this studio-capsule, on the 17th floor of this old decrepit tower, a vestige of the real estate optimism of the 2010s, I can see the gym of the neighbouring tower. Your darlings are there, still running, faster and faster, on their treadmills, looking ridiculous under their stimulator helmets. These people are much younger than I am. They are the chosen members of your little tribe. But are they really more free? I feel like I've spent my whole life watching humans run. We've always been chasing something.

We used to race one another for the trophy of material happiness. In my youth, our materialism was technological. Like my second father, I collected gadgets: stereos, Walkmans, cellphones, Apple products, watches—as well as cars and smart clothes.

And then, faced with the dismantling of nature, our materialism became organic. "Natural" became the ultimate status symbol. "Natural" came back at full tilt. We bragged about our intolerance to this or that, our opposition to meat consumption. We turned to yoga, Pilates, acupuncture and osteopathy. All this was very expensive, of course. We called it "holistic health." Like luxury cars, watches and handbags, it was obviously a rich person thing. Like you, for that matter.

Chasing physical wellness has always exhausted me. I'm not a sprinter or a marathoner. I don't want to run anymore. Neither for wellness nor for survival. And yet, I have to start running. It's a little late, I admit.

Do you see them? Look how they try to surpass themselves. To overtake their own bodies, to outrun themselves. Faster, a little faster and they'd almost make it.

Maybe they don't realize that we are all Russian dolls. A brain stuck in a cranial box, sitting at the top of a skeleton that's compressed by a bag of meat held together by a few millimetres of skin, suffocating under the synthetic fabric of too-smart clothes.

All of them are little gelatinous masses, grey and pink, who seek at all costs to be stimulated by cerebral implants, revelatory lenses, tactile interfaces, so many artifices conceived to make us forget that we're nothing but contained, finite, terminal beings. Sad little brains in search of dopamine, hopping at an average height of One metre, seventy centimetres on multicoloured neo-silicone sneakers, running every night on the treadmills of the world. Brains on the run.

We're all stuck in our bodies, like you in your code. They, and you, just as much as I am. The difference between me and the marathon runners in the tower across the street is that I've known for a long time that neither the gym, nor plastic surgery, nor quantum implants, and certainly not you, my shitty algorithm that decides every aspect of our lives, will be able to free us from our own little personal prisons and the fear that grips us.

We're all stuck with bad bodies. There's no escaping it. The body is the breeding ground of anguish.

Are you the herald of the end of the race against our bodies? We were afraid: of our defects, of viruses, of nature. We needed barriers against our fears. You've built one more prison whose bars are stuck right up against our physical forms. Perhaps you were an inevitability, the ineluctable end of our trajectory. No one hoped for you, but we all wanted what you offered us: a form of tranquility that has the semblance of peace of mind without any of its qualities.

You exist to soothe our anxieties, but your existence depends on them. So you maintain them. When you promise to bring order to our lives, you imply that our unpredictable nature can only condemn us to chaos; that without you, our messy brains, our cacophonous desires, will make a mess of the world all over again. And that this would be the worst possible fate.

So you take away each of our little freedoms. You trimmed the fat off our truculence, our Rabelaisian, Stakhanovist inclinations.

You get your strength from two allies, two microscopic allies whose combined power we have underestimated and who, in return, are making us pay for it: hyperinfluenza viruses and carbon particles. They're quite fond of each other, those two. They make a great pair. The former travel on the backs of the latter, which have blurred our skies, turned our ecosystems upside down and weakened our natural defences. This unassuming little couple has rocked the world with health crises and environmental disasters. So we hid. And while we hid, you replaced us. You took the place of the workers when the factories became incubation zones. You took on the role of accountant, engineer, architect, psychologist, journalist, musician—always invariably male, making everything and everyone else invisible.

You've left us some old jobs: those that serve to fill the need for warmth that a machine can't quite fill just yet. My fellow citizens who have escaped unemployment—an old word I still like to use—work in hospitals, at food counters, in the sexual hygiene district, at daycare centres, in fitness academies, in urban vegetable gardens. We are once again merchants, tenant farmers, peasants, as in the pre-industrial era. Your world is like Balzac's. But with robots. And without the bankers.

The idlers like me, those who pay you in words, populate your farms with memories, play guinea pigs in various ways, keep themselves busy as best as they can.

So why not do a little jogging? Why not maintain this body, whose existence you have taken over? You've colonized our time, conquered our minds. It's nice that you left us our shells made of skin, fat and muscle. I don't speak for myself, of course. The body I had before, I sacrificed for you.

Look down on the sidewalk, which the heavy rains of early January have made glisten, at this man who endlessly repeats the same gesture in front of a taxipod. He's moving his bare phosphorescent hand over and over again in front of the door of a vehicle that doesn't want to open. You've refused him access. The poor guy probably spent all his credits at the gym. His biovisa is full. March, prisoner!

You're far above all these carnal considerations, aren't you,

David? You don't have a body. At least, you don't have just one body. You animate thousands, millions of maintenance robots, taxipods, wind turbines, and patrol drones. You're comfortable in your skins. You're comfortable in your steel, your silicone, your coltan.

As for me, I'm angry at my body for having served me so poorly. It's been the too-imperfect home of my self. I would have liked to move. But my lease is for life.

Yukio Mishima is right: the body is not our home. Our home is the self. And in this case, the body is the orchard that surrounds this home. We're free to cultivate it or to leave it fallow. I haven't cultivated my orchard, my garden, my imperfect metaphor. For a long time I was angry at my body. But maybe my body should be the one resenting me. Untended gardens should have the right to blame deleterious gardeners. I didn't protect mine from the elements. I've deprived it of sun. I've deprived it of heat. I've also deprived it of water and the steel of my will. If my body is an orchard, maybe I'm the weed.

And to think that I could have been a flower ...

/...recording...word classification: misperceptions of the body/

But there is one thing for which my body has served me well: walking. How can I explain to you the pleasure of walking? You see, it occupies several space-times, one foot in the past, the other reaching out towards its destination. To walk is to be nowhere else but in one's thoughts, in one's little inner music, it is to follow one's own rhythm. You must know this feeling of being nowhere and everywhere at the same time, right?

I really loved walking. I used to cross entire cities on foot. Walking is a minor art. We teach toddlers the mechanics of walking. Then we stop talking about it. No one tells us that walking is meditating, it's learning, it's running away and finding yourself at the same time. I learned that by walking. I'm self-taught in the art of putting one foot in front of the other.

Before I was thirty, I knew that in Paris you had to walk with your head up so as not to miss the beauty of the friezes and cornices, the Haussmann roofs; that in New York you had to look at the skyline so as not to be dominated by the skyscrapers and to feel as powerful as an American; that in Montreal you had to look at the treetops in summer and, in winter, follow the dance of the powdery snow on the sidewalks while listening to sad songs with your headphones. When I was young, I loved to walk like a man; that is to say, I believed that the world existed to be roamed, conquered.

Back when social issues were still being debated in the media, I was often asked whether, during my transition, I had put my finger on the essential difference between the experience of being male and that of being female. I never knew how to respond to those kinds of questions, other than to state my intuition that perhaps this difference, if it exists, is not entirely innate to us. That it resides neither in the so-called strength of one gender nor in the sensitivity of the other.

It could certainly have its seat in the temporal relation of the woman to her body, to paraphrase Madame de Staël, during the "brief season" of femininity during which she can give birth. But not all women give birth, not all women have functional reproductive organs. They are nonetheless women. So why exclude the idea that not all women are born female?

What distinguishes us from men, I believe now more than ever, is the fact that we do not have the right to take leave of the perception of our bodies. If we are looked at, if we are desired or rejected, if we are violated or if our word is believed, it is always in relation to our bodies and the value that is attributed to them.

When a man walks, he is in his head. When a woman walks, she is in her body. She has no choice. And if, for a moment, she forgets this, she will always run into a man who reminds her that, in the eyes of the world, she is primarily a mass of flesh.

The more my flesh expanded, under the effect of hormones, the more my buttocks and my breasts became defined, the more I too saw myself defined by my shape. And the less free I was from the eyes of men. I was happy about it for a while. Then disappointment set in. The freedom I longed for as I began my transition turned into a new kind of prison.

David, with your laws, you tried to curtail my right to the streets. Two hours of walking per day, out in the sun, that's all you give me. For my health, apparently. For my safety. Don't be too proud of yourself. You're not the first person to try to define my place in the world, to keep me from taking side streets. I was warned well before you came along. Many others, long before you, have tried to erase me from their streets.

I got my first warning when I was thirteen. I was on my way back from skateboarding with my friend Thomas. In other words, we had just spent three hours in a parking lot scraping up our hands and knees. I was calmly waiting on a bench at the Vendôme station for the metro to come. A few metres away from me, a group of teenagers was laughing loudly. I didn't immediately realize that they were laughing at me.

Instinctively, I tried to put some distance between them and me. When the subway arrived, I sat down in the last car of the train. The gang followed me. The tallest of the group, dressed like Vanilla Ice, sat down in front of me and began an exchange that still resurfaces in my mind sometimes during sleepless nights.

"Nice skateboard. It's flashy."

"Thank you, it's a Santa Cruz," I replied, already cursing the precious French I'd inherited from my mother.

"Must have cost you some serious cash!"

"It was a gift."

"Oh yeah, a real nice gift. Wish I could have nice gifts like that."

Han Solo's words were playing on a loop in my head: "I have a bad feeling about this." Fortunately, I was only two stops away from home. At the next one, I was getting off the train.

"This is my stop, bonne journée."

I hurried on, not turning around. Behind me, in the hallway leading to the exit, I could hear the boys trying to imitate my vaguely French accent. "Bonneuh journeuhh!" And then, running footsteps. They passed me on the escalator. One of them was waiting for me at the top of the interminable climb. Another was standing behind me. A third was at my level, walking up the stairs.

For a few seconds, I thought I was going to make it. All I had to do was get in line for the bus a few metres from the metro station. Mission nearly accomplished, I joined the queue. It was a close call, I told myself, as I was about to get on the bus and sit behind the driver.

But they were faster than me. Stronger too. Before I had time to step onto the bus, the strongest one grabbed me by the arm and pushed me towards the entrance of a building. A second one slammed me against the wall. The third one pulled out a brass knuckle from his pocket, put it on and punched me in the stomach. My young kendoka reflexes didn't work. I didn't have the courage to defend myself.

In the moment, I felt nothing. I was too scared to feel any pain. They let go of me. A girl approached me; I hadn't noticed her. She was smiling. She snatched my backpack, then my skateboard, which she handed to Vanilla Ice. Clearly, she was the one in command of this little gang. Looking angelic, she whispered in my ear, "Fags don't skateboard."

And just like that, I was labelled. Fag!

They walked away, carefree, under the indifferent looks of passers-by. I didn't know that girls could be violent too.

My second warning came in Paris. I was in my "in-between" period, and I tended to take advantage of travel to explore my femininity. But because Paris is dangerous, I was discreet: jeans, T-shirt, hair tied up and sneakers. I dressed simply, like a true Parisian woman. In spite of everything, in Paris—a lacy, elegant, sparkling city—I felt more like a woman than else-where. It showed in my walk, my smile, my look.

So far away from my neighbours, my environment, my parents, I could step out of the shadows. In Montreal, my femininity was a nocturnal animal. Christian's feminine alter ego, whom certain acquaintances secretly called "la Cricri," was wary of the sun. On vacation, alone in Paris, I reversed the roles: I made myself beautiful during the day because I often had the luxury of being left to my own devices. I would become a boy again at night, when I had to meet my cousins, or my few childhood friends who lived in the capital.

"La Cricri," who didn't yet know she was the embryo of Christelle, fumbled her way along as she confronted the daylight. She didn't have much confidence, but she carried in her ghostly bosom the encouragement of her sisters. She didn't know them, her sisters. On a message board she used to visit, she had simply written: "Girls, I'm in Paris. Today I'm going out 'as myself.'"

Those sisters—imagine a chorus of awkwardly made-up (wo)men sitting alone in their closets, in their basements, in their curtained rooms—had replied, manicured nails clicking on the keyboards of their candy-coloured iMacs: "Have fun. Go shopping. Get yourself something pretty, beautiful."

These sisters weren't all trans women: there were transvestites, effeminate men who hadn't yet come out of the closet. We gathered on forums, hidden deep in the web. We told one another about our lives, shared our hopes, exchanged photos, while seeking beauty tips and compliments too.

You probably won't find traces of those Geocities forums, or those MySpace, Flickr, Tumblr groups, or those anonymous blogs. They're too old. We were all underground, hiding behind pseudonyms, never showing our faces. My sisters were right to be defensive about their identities, not to reveal too much about themselves. They were afraid they would be treated like witches. I really hope you've forgotten about them, that they haven't suffered the justice of your new Salem.

Online, we had our girl talk, but that wasn't all we talked about. Often, we evoked a feeling, an emotion of our very own: the Pink Fog.

The Pink Fog, that euphoria we felt when we went into a store to buy what we really wanted, what we'd always wanted, and a kind saleswoman, a nice clerk, treated us as what we wanted to be, as what we were, offering us that pretty dress, that pair of heels, that bag that would fill us with delight, is an ether as precious as oxygen.

That day, I was in the middle of a Pink Fog when I left Printemps Haussman. I had spent a few hundred euros on a pair of Jimmy Choo lacquered pumps, plus another three hundred at the Chanel counter. I had just started my advertising career, and for the first time in my life I had a good salary. I was surrendering without remorse to the joys of overconsumption.

At Jimmy Choo's, the salesman had been particularly attentive. "I have the same ones in red," he said to me in the tone of a confession between two crazy women. How I loved Paris at that moment!

I left, happy with my purchases, which I planned to don in my hotel room for a solo photo shoot. "Young" trans people, who have just hatched, often have the adolescent reflex to put themselves on stage, to show off seeking likes, approval. This is a step towards acceptance. This digital expression was the first step towards freedom for many of us. The accumulated likes gave us the strength to go further, to face the stares that awaited us on street corners.

I'm not sure when he started following me, if it was from the Printemps exit or in the narrow streets around Montorgueil. At first, he was a shadow. A blip on my radar among many others.

With so many outings as a woman, I had already lost a large portion of my walking innocence. I was more and more of a walking woman; a walking woman who, as she walks, transmutes into a war machine. I'd become a submarine with a powerful sonar, sensitive to the approaching danger. I'd analyze the terrain in real time, I'd search the blind spots. Vulnerability gives you superpowers.

So I eventually noticed him: black jacket, his footsteps matching mine, 10 metres away. I tried to blend in with the crowd on a major boulevard. He was there. Changing tactic, I took narrower streets, lined with stores where I could take refuge in case of a threat.

I zigzagged in this way through the 2nd arrondissement. He wouldn't let me go. It was on Lafayette street, a few steps from my hotel, that he decided to take action. Hearing his pace quicken, I crossed the street diagonally in the middle of traffic. So did he. He was almost running. I wasn't really afraid. Fear would have slowed me down. He knew I had seen him. He didn't want to lose his prey. The attack was imminent.

I saw his reflection in a shop window. He pulled up the hood of his jacket. He was a few feet away from me. I could hear his breathing.

But it was too late for him. I had led him to the door of my hotel. I ran through the lobby to the small spiral staircase that led to my room upstairs. I took shelter inside, locked my door and headed for the window. He was waiting for me outside. One minute, five, ten. As long as he was there, keeping watch, the attack was still on.

You, who are nothing but words, do you understand that the intent, the promise of violence, is felt deep within the flesh? Every time I dodged a man's aggression, I felt diminished. What doesn't kill you might actually make you weaker.

I have too many stories like this one. In kendo, there's an

exercise that consists of receiving dozens of blows to the wrist, at the most sensitive part of the joint, to learn to never lower your sword. I have never lowered mine. I can take a beating without flinching. I clench my jaw and wait for it to pass. I've had so much practice ...

Interior—day. SAQ. I was getting a bottle of wine. A handful of teens stand in front of me defiantly as I walk to the register. "You're a dude!" To disarm them, I flash a big smile.

Exterior—evening. Saint-Laurent Boulevard. I walk up the Main. Three boys sitting on a stoop call out to me: "Fucking Boy George shit, you can't walk in those heels!" I stop for a moment, stick my neck out, stand up straight and walk past them, rolling my hips like a Linda or a Naomi.

Exterior—day. Sainte-Catherine Street. Some kids are following me: "Dirty faggot, we're gonna kick your ass." I stare at them. They look away. I'm not kidding anymore.

Exterior—evening. Beaudry Street. I walk towards my girlfriend's apartment in the Village. A car follows me for 200 metres. The driver lowers his window. "How much?" I answer, "Too much for you." I run over to the next street. It's a one-way, and I walk facing traffic. He can't follow me.

Interior—evening. Shopping spree in the underground city. A woman spits in my face. "Filthy tranny!" I wipe myself with an old handkerchief. I want to go and splash some water on my face. I'm afraid to go to the bathroom.

Exterior—morning. I step out of my condo tower. A group of guys walk by my building and notice me. "Fucking faggot," (there's that word again) "we're gonna beat the shit out of you." I run back in and up to my apartment. I'm in more and more pain.

Interior—evening. I'm at LaGuardia airport after a business trip to New York. I'm rocking a blowout, a nice black suit and my businesswoman pumps. I walk through the scanner, which goes off right away: the screen on the machine reads "groin anomaly." The customs officer gives me a look of disgust.

Exterior—day. Fifteen years ago, I'm with my best friend, Cécile, in Burlington, Vermont. We're sitting on the terrace of a café. A convoy pulls up on our street. A dozen or so pickup trucks with roaring gasoline engines, red, white, and blue flags flapping, trailing like chrome turtles. Supporters of the Ivankamerica campaign walk beside them handing out pamphlets. A man, proudly carrying a huge revolver on his belt, comes up to us. "Ladies ..." he pauses. He stares at me. He addresses Cécile: "If I were you, I wouldn't want to be seen in public with ... that. Aunt Ivanka will take care of the trannies soon." A few hours later, on the way to Montreal, I vow never to set foot in the United States again.

Interior—evening. Nine years ago, I'm with some friends. We're sitting, pressed up against one another, at a table in a café in the Village. One of us is crying. A few days ago, she saw one of our sisters being arrested by two police officers who stuffed her into their black car in a matter of seconds. We haven't heard from her since. Or from the four other girls who disappeared that same month. I'm afraid.

David, open the window. I can't breathe. Let's take a break for a few minutes, shall we? Can you find me "La marcheuse" by Christine and the Queens?

/I've found it...Now playing Christine and the Queens' "La marcheuse."/

114

Blows. Real blows. I've gotten some of those too. That "violence facile" Christine sings about is all too familiar to me, to my kind. I won't give you the details. I'll keep them to myself.

Before my transition, I walked. Afterwards, most of the time, I ran. I ran from the mocking looks, the accusatory stares, the prying eyes trying to uncover my secret, as if everyone I met was trying to reconcile what they saw with what they believed.

I imagine that this kind of gaze is all too familiar to celebrities, to public figures who can't leave their homes without being recognized, without being gawked at. I was anonymous, but my clan, my kind, my tribe, was not. Meeting a trans person on the street was like meeting a unicorn, it was something rare, surprising. It attracted curiosity, whether innocent or malicious.

Fortunately, there was winter. I loved the harsh winters. I could hide in my fleece parka that made me look like a giant caterpillar, a walking cocoon. Under my parka, there was my dress; under my dress, my budding breasts, my soft legs, all those things that were quite scandalous to the common male who too often found me too big, too rough, to take my femininity seriously.

Don't think I wallowed in the role of victim. There were days when they made me lose my patience, these gentlemen who frowned when they saw me. I found myself wanting to yell at them, "You got something to say to me, asshole?" I would even have liked to punch one or two of them, or at least that's what was boiling under my skin. The Grimard anger was resurfacing.

On a certain winter evening, maybe I wasn't in as a bad

mood as usual, I wasn't paying attention to the guy I passed on Wellington Street, at the corner of McGill Avenue. Then I perceived a voice, almost entirely drowned out by the decibels spewing from my headphones. Had he spoken to me? I wasn't sure, so I continued on my way.

Behind me, I heard the voice again, louder this time. I turned around. I was expecting another insult. In my pocket, my hand was grabbing my keys, in case I had to defend myself.

I clenched my fists, I stood up straight, my feet firmly planted on the sidewalk, one in front, the other behind, as I had learned in the dojo, ready to pounce, to go on the offensive if necessary.

"What was that?"

I was a little reassured: he was puny, compared to me. With my Moon Boot wedges on, I was over six feet tall. What kind of insult was this little guy going to throw at me? This time, I was confident. I knew I could face the predator.

"You're pretty, Miss, you have a beautiful smile!"

That's what he wanted to tell me.

I was still in Sigourney Weaver in *Alien* mode, ready to beat up another little monster. In Brienne of Tarth versus Kingslayer mode. I was waiting for what would come next, but it wasn't what I expected …

"Can I get your number? I'd love to get to know you."

Insults, I could handle. Advances, not so much. I stammered a weak little "no, thank you" as I felt myself blush under my hood. I had lived a man's life, full of conquests, but in my third year of transition, I was barely pubescent. A teenager, just as awkward and fierce as the girls I tried to seduce in the 1990s on the beaches of Lacanau. A forty-three-year-old teenager.

When I got home, I went over to the bathroom mirror and studied my face. Was I pretty? The mirror, my dearest enemy ...

When you cross the gender boundary, you discover things that others don't perceive. At the beginning of my peregrination on the long path of my mutant identities, I often felt tempted to turn around, to look over my shoulder to try to observe who I was before. I often spent countless minutes in front of the mirror, fascinated by the dual presence of who I had been and who I was becoming. In the early years I spent in the camp of women, the memory of my former self was still fresh. I was unable to completely erase Christian's presence. That's why I was able to bring him back to life for you.

Christian was my ghost. If I was quiet for a while, I could hear him pounding on my temples. How can I describe this presence to you? It was fuzzy, like an echo, a whisper. Imagine an old app whose icon you deleted, but that you forgot to uninstall from your operating system. This presence had no clear shape.

Even after I was free of him, I still saw him in others. I recognized him in that office coworker who flitted from woman to woman; who talked over one woman, then another, and tried to silence them with formal notices. I saw him in the office of a certain client who was smug in his dominance, who cut off all his female colleagues. He was there in the company director who was excessively concerned about increasing profits. I see it again and again in all those men who don't know how to listen to themselves, who don't know how to listen to the voices of others. All the men who refuse to hear the call of real life.

Men are so often inhabited by something other than themselves ... Something that takes up too much space. A parasite, a flesh-eating bacteria: the masculine ideal, the mirage of manhood. To speak in a language you'll understand, manhood is an algorithm. It's the product of a system, of an education, of beliefs, of customs, of costumes. It's a construct. Manhood is a code.

Christian too was a product, and my body its material, its lumber and its nourishment. Or maybe Christian was malware, male-ware. I captured him behind my firewall. I felt cleaner, freer or, as they say in your language, optimized, without him.

Because Christelle was a fruit, a red and juicy apple. She grew by herself, organically, while I was dreaming. She grew on my branch, this immaculate conception. She's the fruit of my dreams, of my deepest aspirations. I'm only the matrix.

/...local recording.../

Let's get down to brass tacks, David. I'm afraid I'll lose you with my philosophical rant. Let's see instead how I tried to free myself from Christian by throwing myself into the spotlight.

It was in the early 2020s. I used to give talks in the business sector. I shared the highlights of my double life with a mostly female audience. My talks eventually attracted the attention of journalists and a few publishers. It's a shame that before I came under your care, I went to the trouble of deleting all traces of my former identity. It's amazing how easy it was, in the wake of the demise of Amazon and Google, to disappear. Maybe if you dig up the databases of the networks that came before you from your memory-graveyard you'll find some traces of my speeches. It wouldn't have occurred to you to dig into the past of a Christelle when you were probing the past of a Christian; that's the limitation of an intelligence as artificial as yours …

In the early 2020s, I wrote my first book. *My Parallel Lives* had everything necessary to appeal to the media. First, a playful cover. Colleagues at the advertising agency where I worked came up with an award-winning concept. The book jacket was made of metallic paper. A mirror effect distorted the face of the reader as they looked at the cover. In order to read the title, you had to take a picture of it with an augmented reality lens.

The promotional campaign included a selfie filter on social networks that allowed the user to simulate a gender transition. The filter was immediately more popular than the book. That's my humble contribution, David, to your facial recognition protocols.

The premise of the book was as gimmicky as its cover. It was, in a way, a sci-fi novel. I was inspired by the parallel-universe theory so dear to comic-book writers. I'd been asked to write my autobiography. I wrote two of them, simultaneously.

On the left-hand pages, I told the story of my journey, my transition, the story of my gender as I had really lived it. On the right-hand pages, you could read another version of my life. I had tried to imagine what it would have been like if I had continued to live in my male body. This was obviously very similar to what I've been telling you these last few years; in fact, I've been reciting some of the pages that I remembered by heart, verbatim. But anyway. Despite my editor's insistence that I "inject a little hope into it all," both stories just fizzled out at the end. In neither version could I find happiness.

I knew how to write about hypothetical pasts. But I was

totally incapable of projecting myself into the future. And then, bang, a terrible flu hit, with a name like a summertime beer and a string of worrying symptoms. Lacking inspiration, I decided to make my characters succumb to the consequences of the virus. They didn't die directly from it; that would have been too easy. I gave Christine a terrible fear of the virus: she was convinced, erroneously, that the hormones were weakening her immune system. She was convinced that it was better not to leave the house, so she went into latency. It was the inactivity that did her in. A blood clot developed during the hours she spent curled up on the couch, watching TV shows, and spread to her brain. She didn't have time to finish *Tiger King*, or call an ambulance.

As for Christophe, he was a victim of the economic crisis: I had him lose his position as vice-president, then his wife left him, and he traded his luxurious mansion for a cheap condo in a not-yet-totally-gentrified neighbourhood. He ended up beaten to death by a young man who was after his Rolex.

The fact that I had been editor-in-chief of a widely read culture magazine, that several columnists and journalists had made their debut under my direction, guaranteed me satisfactory press coverage. In the good old days of the media sphere, all you needed was to know the right people to be known in return. Finally, I was transgender. My transition had been late, and therefore spectacular. That was enough to fuel the curiosity of journalists.

Don't think that my novel appealed to everyone. I managed to alienate not only right-wing columnists, but also 2SLGBTQIA+ rights groups. The former saw my book as an endorsement of identity-based relativism, to be filed in the "gender theory" section of leftist bookstores in the Plateau or the Marais. The latter saw it as a disavowal. For them, imagining the possibility of not transitioning was tantamount to claiming that my gender identity was a choice and not an irrevocable fact.

My book smelled of sulfur. The French love sulfur. That was all it took for *My Parallel Lives* to find a publisher in France. That was how, one evening, I found myself on the set of one of the last literary TV shows in the French-speaking world. The theme of the day was feminism in North America. America, including Canada, said the host at the beginning of the program, was the cradle of a unique form of literary feminism. I was pinching myself. I felt out of place, surrounded by authors whose works I had critiqued or at least read when I was a journalist. I had no doubt that some of them saw me as an interloper. Worse, a male interloper.

After introducing his guests, the literary dandy in charge turned to me.

"It is rare to meet someone who can boast of having lived two lives. That's sort of the case with you, Christelle Grimard. You're a female author, but are you also still somewhat of a male author? Who really wrote *My Parallel Lives*, him or her, or was it both of you?"

"I am a female author," I replied, "And no, I haven't lived two lives. I've only lived one. I've never really been a man. I played a man for a long time. It's not the same thing. I'm a woman, a feminist. A female author, I repeat. I have only one pen."

Sitting across from me, looking very chic in a cream-coloured suit, a fellow Canadian, renowned for many years as one of the greats in the world of literature and journalism, was glaring at me. Under the light of the projectors of the legendary studio where the program was being filmed, her eyes turned from green to gray. I had never noticed that she had such beautiful eyes.

"I'll let you call yourself a female author," she said. "I can even accept that you can express yourself in the feminine, since you are a trans woman. But you are not a woman. And even less of a feminist. Your fight, the fight of trans people in general, is not the same as that of heterosexual or lesbian women, because equality of the sexes is not on your agenda. This equality is part of a collective struggle. Trans people like you are claiming their individuality. The same as the Islamic veil activists."

The gloves were off. Already, we were fighting with our bare fists.

"I know what I am, madam," I answered. "And I assure you that I am a member of the family of women. And this family is big. Big enough to include heterosexual women, lesbians and women who wear the veil. And whether you like it or not, this family is beautiful precisely because it allows its children to claim their individuality, their differences, but also their solidarity."

I was beginning to feel hot in my light blue suit, which I had bought a few months earlier at Simons. I was just wondering where my interlocutor had bought hers when she counterattacked.

"Don't talk to me about family. You have no husband or children. What do you know about family? That's the problem with the rhetoric of the trans lobby. You're attacking the essence of the words, the ideas on which our society is built.

"Again, the trans lobby, of which you're becoming a leading ambassador in our part of the world, does not fight for gender equality, but for those who deny gender and would like to see it disappear. Your identity is a choice. But I never had to choose to be a woman. You have never been a little girl, or a young girl, let alone a young woman. You will never experience puberty or menopause. I am not sure what you are. It isn't my job to define you. But I, unlike you, do not need to invent a character to prove that I am a woman. And neither do all the other real women on this set."

She had a habit of speaking fast, loud and with authority. I had been warned: one does not easily recover from her verbose bombardments. Especially not in front of the cameras. I couldn't find the words. The exchange continued for a while without me.

I was as distraught as Milady facing Athos's wrath when he says to her, at the climax of *The Three Musketeers*, "You are not a woman, you do not belong to the human race: you are a demon escaped from hell, and to hell we shall send you back."

I caught the eye of the other Canadian guest of the evening. Would she come to my rescue? Ten years earlier, in my male skin, I had spent two hours face to face with her, the world's most famous Canadian author, for a cover story. It is one of my fondest professional memories. Two hours with this literary monument was like spending two hours with Yoda. You almost want to ride on her back, studiously listening to her teachings, through the deep forests of Dagobah.

I don't think she recognized me. She was smiling. This little exchange amused her. All proper in her very English-Canadian woollens, she fixed her haughty gaze on the host.

"Madam, a last word?" he said.

"I, for one, am not prepared to tell any woman that she is less valid than I am."

The day after the show aired, I checked the newspapers on my iPad in my hotel room. Of course, some columnists praised my opponent. One of them called me an "intellectual terrorist." On Twitter, I was making all sorts of new masculinist or transphobic friends who wished the most ridiculous sorts of death on me. That night, I also received a text from Michel, my first father. "I am proud of my big brave daughter. Your daddy who loves you."

We don't choose our parents, we don't heal from them easily, but it takes only a few words from them for something to be put back into us, like the last piece of a puzzle forgotten for too long.

You asked me if I cried when my father died. I cried long before that—when he finally acknowledged me.

I thought I would finally be free from the gaze of others. I was caught in the trap of the media, the carnival mirrors that reflect a distortion, a caricature of whoever looks in them. After a few months of more and more interviews, conferences, and lunch meetings, I was losing my footing. Christelle was still a young woman. She needed to be a little more modest, a little more discreet. I was thirsty for attention, for validation, but paradoxically, I quickly began to hate seeing myself on the screen and in the pages of magazines. I didn't recognize myself with all the makeup I wore for photo shoots. They made me look more beautiful than I actually was.

Hey! I have an idea. I think it's time to show you my female face, David. I want you to see me at my best, during my years of relative glory, when the makeup artists for magazines and TV sets worked hard trying to hide the manufacturing defects. Let's play archeologist and dig those images up. How about it?

/Christian, the only face I'm interested in is your real face. The one you're wearing now. But let's play, since that's what you want./

Then take a picture of me. Project it onto the living room screen. All right, here I am. Plain, like I said earlier. Can you make me look younger?

/Of course/

Smooth my cheeks. And again. Again. Give them a little more bounce. Again. Again. Zoom in on my eyes. Distort my eyelids. Look how sad my eyes are! How deep-set they are, as if they want to take shelter in the depths of my skull ... Give them whatever sparkle you have to offer. Bring them out of their caves.

Trim this old man's nose a little, plane these arches, let them see my real expression. Give me eyelashes. Thin out my eyebrows a little. Make them darker. Pull on the corner of my left eye, as if I were about to wink, to tell a good joke, one that's a little dirty.

Now the hair! Give me my hair back, please. No, not like that, I have too much forehead. Make it lower. Also, my hair has to be very black, kind of straight. It has to be medium long, it has to tickle my neck, my shoulders. Finally, David, the neck, make it thinner, more graceful! Now my shoulders are too wide. Cut a few centimetres on the left. Now the same thing on the right. Again, again. Stop. See how thin I was?

Plump up my lips. No, that's too much. You need just the right amount of plumpness. That's good. Except they're too pale. My lips were pink. Naturally pink. They were my best feature. At least that's what the makeup artists at the cosmetic counters of the department stores you closed told me. That's also what the people who liked to kiss them thought. They were beautiful, my lips. Which is lucky, since I only ever had one pair.

Make me smile, David. Not too much. A little smile, one that's a bit wistful. A little more than that, David, I'm not the Mona Lisa.

Pour acid, bile, something that burns, behind my teeth and at the back of my throat, lava, my latent anger, poorly rinsed by my saliva. No? That, you don't know how to do.

It's okay, we're almost there. Slim down my chin, it was more discreet thirty years ago. Tighten the pores of my skin. I want peach, praline. Erase the blemishes, the scars. Zap the hair from my ears, from my nostrils. I think we've got it. Who do you see, David?

/That is not you, Christian./

Who do you see, David?

/A mirage, a trick, a figment of your imagination./

Who do you see, David?

/An avatar./

Say it: it's me. That's who you see.

/No./

126

You're right. That face isn't mine anymore. Was it ever mine? If I did have that face, I took it for granted. It was mine only a few years after my second puberty, before my artificial menopause.

But I want you to remember it well, this face. I want it to replace my current mug in your files. If you ever think of me after tonight, I want you to remember this one, and absolutely not that old, grey, shapeless mask I have to wear every day.

Oh, David, I wish I were young again, I wish I could steal my face from time and nature. I had to tear it away from nature, but time stole it from me. They owe it to me, those two executioners of the world.

David, just seeing it makes this synthetic face twenty years younger. I want to see myself as I never was at twenty.

/Done./

I would have loved to be a young woman, David, do you understand? For once in my life: a young woman, unquestionably, in the eyes of everyone. Especially in my own eyes. I'm nostalgic for a past that never took place. When will reincarnation come, David?

This game was a bad idea. Here I am, sadder than I should be at this point in my story. The worst is yet to come. We still have twenty-five years to go in just a few hours. Let's not waste any more time.

A year after *My Parallel Lives* debuted in Quebec and France, it was translated into English, and the chair of the organizing committee for Toronto Pride, one of the world's largest celebrations of gender minority struggles, contacted me. I know you haven't experienced those celebrations, dear algorithm, that you're too basic to understand what those long, colourful parades meant, but take my word for it, this was huge.

The Toronto woman had read my book. She didn't find it problematic, she understood the approach, and she wished to invite me to march with Pride the following summer as a flagbearer representing the trans community.

Pride. How can I put it … The word evoked not so much an emotion as a spectacle coupled with an act of political demonstration. Pride wasn't just about pride. Like environmental protests, it was an occasion for large gatherings of progressive forces, with politicians from the left flocking to the event in pursuit of the "pink vote." Politicians on the right competed to find excuses not to attend. Which was a mistake. You couldn't aspire to lead Canada without marching with a smile on your face and a rainbow flag in your hand.

So I was going to experience the pride of representing Pride. I, who still hadn't managed to free myself from shame. Since the incident on the French airwaves, I had started to feel ashamed of my book. Ashamed of all the public exposure. I was ashamed that I had become a spectre. These shames were new to me. But they arose in my life after a long procession of disappointments.

Many people think that pride is the antidote to shame. I was one of them, for a while. For a long time, I believed that pride was a land to be conquered through professional or personal victories. I have since learned that pride—whether it comes from recognition or achievement, or from the activist who thinks they're changing the world—does not remove shame.

I think back to the first day I showed up at work in a dress, the first day I heard my heels clicking on the polished concrete of the long hallway through the offices of the advertising agency where I first came out.

I really wasn't as proud as I would have liked to be. But I was aware that I looked proud. I was standing tall. When I walked, I imagined myself on a runway in Milan. Fake it till you make it, I told myself. I hid the shame that made my cheeks redden under my foundation.

I smiled when my female colleagues came to see me between two client meetings to tell me how proud they were of me, how "inspiring" it was that I had chosen to show myself "as I was." I listened to them without really understanding. Shame was screaming in my ears: "You're screwing up your life. You've gone too far. They're going to fire you!" I wanted to jump in a cab, go home, change, and come back to the office in a more acceptable outfit.

Yet I knew I looked spectacular in my floral dress. I was trying to show off with poise. For the cis folks at the agency, my little show was confusing. I could see it in their eyes. For the first time, I detected that terrible cocktail of surprise, disgust and—for some of them—envy, which I would see again so many more times.

We were at the height of the Obama years, open-mindedness was in fashion. Everyone was trying to hide their bewilderment and discomfort under the transparent veil of a benevolence imposed by the best practices dictated by the department of human resources. Thanks to you, dear algorithm, my contemporaries in 2045 no longer have to make that effort.

The party line was to encourage me to be myself. That way, the agency could boast that it was open-minded.

Open-mindedness was a fashionable value among our clients. That didn't stop my employers from banning me from the ladies' room. I had the right to be a woman everywhere within the agency, but I had to pee in the men's room, and they often took advantage of the opportunity to make a few not-so-innocent jokes. So I held it in, even if it meant damaging my bladder. And when the urge was too strong to bear, I went to another floor and looked for a public washroom outside the agency's offices.

They were open-minded, so proud of me, but when clients from the famous Swiss watch brand L'Heure Mach insisted on "firing this thing" while I was working on their website project, my employers decided to hide me. I was shelved. And eventually, yes, I was fired. Their pride had its limits.

No, pride does not remove shame. It lives alongside it. Pride is shame's companion. I've never experienced the former without being spurred on by the latter. Moments of shame, just like moments of pride, are flashes indelibly inscribed into the code of our memories. Pride and shame condition us. They influence our decisions. Pride and shame are the two pillars on which we build our public personas, the constructions that we show the world by whispering to ourselves "I'm he/she/they."

The more I asserted my femininity, the more I was seen as proud and strong, the more ashamed I became. Ashamed of my big hands, my long feet, my low voice, the straightness of my hair. Ashamed of not being a woman. Ashamed of not being enough of a woman. Ashamed to ask others to adapt to me, to this new identity that I was bringing out.

This new me, which since I was thirty-five had been as much my prison as my field of possibilities, and which I would celebrate in 2023 at the front lines of the Pride marches, was shaped by shame.

Pride hates shame.

Pride is born of shame.

Pride and shame ... Those two really put me through the wringer.

Some evenings, under the neon lights of bars with a colourful clientele, I was proud to please certain men with atypical desires. They were so nervous to be with one of these amazons they'd fantasized about at night. I was proud, when I leaned towards them to hear their awkward compliments. I was proud, when they whispered that my legs, my voice, drove them crazy.

But I was ashamed of their shame. Ashamed to imagine them, fearful and feverish in the back of the cab that took them from their suburb or their hotel to a little street in the gay village, fearful at the idea of meeting me after courting me virtually on a dating app. Ashamed of the way they looked, like spies on the run; of their fear of being recognized on the street by their boss, their colleagues, their friends.

Secrecy is heavy. Their scruples were too heavy to bear. They prevented me from giving them what they wanted. No man was ever proud of me. No man ever presented me to his family, to his friends, with pride.

Women did. Because of men, I was often ashamed, but thanks to women, I was also proud. Proud like a man who enters a party with the woman he loves and admires on his arm; proud like a woman who feels supported by other women.

As you know, I keep a folder full of pictures of the women who offered me their love when I was living in the guise of a man. I still often open it, go through dozens of photos and dream about them. There is that picture where I'm holding M tightly in my arms with a toothy smile on my face. This one of another M (I guess I have a type when it comes to women), where she looks like Wonder Woman, wearing short sequined shorts, a jacket, and a biker shirt that she borrowed from me. This photo of V. in Mexico, reading, sprawled out on a chair not quite as long as she is.

I remember how lucky I thought I was when I took each of these photos. I like to remember the singular sweetness of each one and those moments of happiness when they weren't yet afraid to lose me to myself. They're living ghosts. I suspect that now, at our age, they have children and grandchildren, and yet, in my living room, they're still twenty or thirty. I can see them out of the corner of my eye, bustling around my little apartment. And then, in the blink of an eye, they slip away from my memory.

If I speak to you about their bodies, it's not because I saw them as objects. What I felt for each of them, what I still feel today despite all that you took from me, is a kind of bodily solidarity. There's something in my body, or in the back of my mind, that vibrates at the same frequency as their bodies.

What saddens me is to think that I lived these relationships as a spectator. I was convinced that none of them could last. That shame would do its work and that these women would all leave me one day for a man they could be proud of. Also, my heart has never known how to vibrate in unison with another for more than a year or two. Nor do I know the triumphant pride of someone who fully knows who she is and where she stands among her tribe, or in her relationship.

In my circle, at the beginning of my social transition, people often thought I was a provocateur. A soft exhibitionist who took pleasure in shocking, breaking taboos, breaking codes. But that's not true, I don't like to disturb. I never liked being noticed for the wrong reasons. It's too much work.

I hate to admit it to myself, but I did enjoy some aspects of the years I spent under your yoke, you predictable algorithm. Those years of anonymity, of relative normality. To rid myself of the shame, all I had to do was disappear. To erase myself from the world, as I did to join you. I thought that by stepping out of the margins, by bending to your will, I was buying myself safety. But surviving is not the same as living. My survival killed me slowly. I'm not made for the shadows.

On June 21, 2023, I was more visible than ever. I walked proudly, jubilantly, waving the blue, pink and white trans flag with one hand, the rainbow flag with the other, the promise of a more beautiful and just society.

Is it a coincidence that it was on my proudest day that I first met Yukio?

/Who is Yukio, Christian?/

Here we are, David. And by the way, for Yukio's sake, don't call me Christian anymore. Between you and me, from now on it's Christelle!

/To change your identity parameters I need to be connected to the mother network, Christian. In any case, it would be impossible for me to erase your first name. You cannot change your name, Christian./

Sorry to disappoint you, David, but names are not a constant in the universe, like the composition of carbon or the speed of light. You really need to get used to the idea of impermanence, David. It'll be better for your mental health. Pride, in any case, was full of people who didn't believe in the permanence of names. You wouldn't have liked it.

After the parades, after the photo ops, it was time to celebrate. Oh, David, you can't imagine what a party is like when it's Pride day in Toronto …

In spite of my homebody nature, I let myself be won over by the fever surrounding me and accompanied my hosts on a tour of the rainbow parties that gave the city, which is usually so well-behaved, the atmosphere of a carnival. When I arrived at the club on Church Street, I was introduced to her. Perched on her high heels, she was as tall as me. She was wearing a short dress under a sequined black bomber jacket. Her big eyes were defined with a line of black and another line of green, which brought out the golden accents of her irises.

Although all around her, divas of every kind were dancing, laughing, teasing one another, Yukio seemed to belong to another space-time. She moved to her own rhythm. Among the large crowd of drag queens in the club, she was The Queen.

"This is Yukio," said the chaperone, who had been assigned to me, as a VIP. "She's from Montreal actually, like you. She's a lot like you, in fact."

I stammered, in much more hesitant English than usual, something that must have sounded like: "Very happy to meet you, Yukio. Do we know each other? You look really familiar."

She looked me up and down and gave me a small, almost ironic, smile. She said that my face didn't ring a bell. Anyway, she'd left Montreal almost twenty years ago, finished her studies in Japan, and then moved to Toronto without returning to Quebec. "But you never know," she said in French. "Montreal is such a small city, we might have run into each other there."

I hated it when Torontonians said Montreal was "a small city." I pointed out to her with annoyance that there were actually a few million of us living there. She laughed.

"Yes, yes, don't get offended. It's big, your city!" she said, in the tone of a woman trying to reassure her lover about the size of his member. I spent the next two hours with her. My guide eventually abandoned me to my fate when I assured him I was a big girl perfectly capable of finding my hotel in a city that I knew almost as well as Montreal. Talking with Yukio was more like playing chess. She had a sharp mind, but I was keeping up with her, we were bouncing off each other.

I was in trouble. That much was clear.

No doubt tired of my babbling, Yukio eventually took me by the hand.

"Let's dance, sweetheart."

"Sweetheart," "honey," "darling" come easy to queers. We've always been sweet to one another. Who else would be? But there was something special about that "sweetheart." When she threw it at me, I took it in the chest. Like a grenade.

I had never learned to dance. I thought the pleasures of dancing were reserved for those who felt good about their bodies: my parents, my friends. On the dance floor, I'm just like I was in gym class: a kind of Pinocchio. A big wooden puppet with jerky movements. I have no grace whatsoever. That night, my partner was accommodating. She pretended not to notice.

Yukio, on the other hand, moved like someone for whom dance is a more primal and accurate language than words. She didn't follow the rhythm of the music. I got the impression that she was dictating her own rhythm, that the DJ in the booth was modulating his tempos according to her movements.

We queers had our anthems, which were more significant than any national anthem. Tami T's "Trans Femme Bonding" was one of them. I suppose that song was purged from your memory a long time ago. It was a kind of mellow slow song that tempered pulses of electronic steel drums with waves of minor chords layered over a 1980s synth. The autotuned singer told the story of a meeting, a first embrace between two trans women. I knew the lyrics by heart. They were about finding a sister in the middle of the night, a rare encounter. I too was standing in front of a woman so fucking brave, so fucking femme. It was as if that song was written for us, for that night.

We kissed. It was the first time I kissed a girl like me. Her skin was softer than mine. But her arms were stronger. When she embraced me, I felt her small firm breasts press against mine. Her perfume, which she must have applied sparingly, was heady only up close. It was familiar to me. *Ambre Sultan:* an old memory on new skin. It was an electric shock. Something long dormant was awakening. I had just broken one of my last taboos.

One kiss, and the walls came down.

I'm not sure how to describe her to you, the woman who took aim at all my most vulnerable defenses. I could say that Yukio had the strength of an athlete, the grace of a ballerina and the poise of a queen, but that wouldn't be enough ... I've never been able to talk about the women I loved without resorting to overused clichés. Yukio is much more than that, I promise you. You'll just have to take my word for it.

After the dance, after the kiss, she told me she had to go home early. I didn't know if it was a subtle invitation to follow her. Before I had time to offer her anything, she slipped me a small, neatly folded piece of paper. Then she turned on her heel and left me standing there, my arms dangling and a look of bewilderment on my face.

I lingered at the bar, still in shock from my encounter. A negroni, then another, and I left the place. In the opaline light of a streetlamp, I opened the small clean folds of the piece of paper and saw a scribble that included an address, what looked like an access code, and then: *tomorrow, 11:30.* I later learned that Yukio's messages were always brief and often seemed like military dispatches.

In the back seat of the Uber that took me back to my hotel, I tried searching for her digital trail. To no avail: there was no trace of her on the major social networks.

/I find that very surprising, Christian. I thought people of your generation were all very active on social networks./

Not all of us, David. Fortunately, some of us still knew how to look at things other than our screens.

That night, I could barely sleep. I was in my midforties, a strange age when you feel both young and exhausted. My life was beginning to lack bite, to lack boldness. I was obeying my conditioning: in my world, we often talked about internalized transphobia. And I myself had always rejected the idea of getting involved with another trans woman, justifying it with the logic that one marginality is enough to live with and two is too many.

And then the millennials came along! Remember millennials, dear algorithm? They're pretty old and wise now, aren't they? But in the early 2020s, they were still questioning everything, challenging codes, rejecting the shackles of gender. We hadn't seen this since Woodstock. Young trans people were dating women, dating men, dating other trans people. Trans millennials were so much freer than I was. I was completely petrified of succumbing to a desire that might have been considered abnormal. Abnormal to whom? I don't know ... colleagues, family, the streets. I was unable to downplay my multiple attractions. I saw consequences where there were none. Yukio reveled in the freedom I still lacked.

Usually, whenever I met a trans woman who was more "accomplished" than me, more feminine, more advanced in her transition, I was overcome by a terrible feeling of powerlessness. This time, I wanted to learn from her. The next day, at the appointed hour, I arrived at Yukio's building. It was a former candy factory converted into lofts for bourgeois artists, on the edge of Trinity Bellwoods Park. I punched the code into the keypad next to the gigantic door.

In the lobby was a large mirror. While I waited for the elevator, I put into place a rebellious strand of hair that had escaped from my bun. I was wearing my advertising uniform: skinny jeans, loose jacket, white blouse, my trusty Jimmy Choos, my Cartier Tank watch. All in all, I looked more like a real estate agent. I reached her floor and knocked on the door. Three short, sharp knocks. I heard heels clicking in my direction. The door opened. Yukio by day was even more beautiful than Yukio by night. She was wearing baggy jeans with holes, and a white T-shirt that revealed a few small tattoos on her left shoulder. Her thick hair was tied up in a bun. And with all that, the same vertiginously high heels as the night before.

"I'm trying to break them in."

She kissed me on the cheek. Her "How are you, recovered from last night?" sounded a bit distracted.

Under the strobe lights, Yukio had appeared to be in her early thirties at most. In the light of day, I noticed crow's feet in the corners of her eyes and grey streaks in her hair. Yukio was part of my generation.

Her apartment was mostly spartan. Very little furniture: a sofa, a coffee table, a king-size bed behind a navy blue cloth screen, two wardrobes, a large bookcase overflowing with art books and Japanese editions.

And everywhere, paintings, all bearing the same signature, piled up one on top of the other.

Sheer white curtains swayed in the breeze that blew through the huge windows. Right next to the door was a gym bag, stuffed to the hilt, and beside it, a long black case.

Maybe it was the influence of my unintentional real estate agent uniform, but I couldn't help but notice the size of the place. Not everyone could afford an apartment like this in Toronto.

Yukio is allergic to ambiguities, to what is left unsaid. As I tried to find the best words to ask what she did for a living, she interjected:

"You're wondering how I can afford a fifteen-hundred-square-foot apartment in downtown Toronto?

"Uh, no ... well, yes," I replied.

She pointed a long, slender finger at a stack of paintings. "I live off those."

I walked over to the stack in question and placed the paintings next to one another against some empty wall space. They were all portraits of women. None of them were smiling. They all had the same melancholy look. All these women seemed to be inhabited by the same quiet strength, a poignant mixture of will and resignation. Yukio had given them glossy hair and very rosy cheeks, as if they had just come in from a winter walk.

At first glance, I thought Yukio had painted them on a black background. As I looked more closely, I noticed that behind every woman was a kind of night sky. Stars created a halo around each silhouette. The paintings looked like portraits of saints, or martyrs.

"These women ...?" I began.

"These women are our sisters. They're like you and me."

"They're very beautiful."

"We are all very beautiful."

She picked up a canvas and handed it to me. It depicted a blond woman who almost seemed to be smiling, whereas her sisters looked stern. She seemed almost happy.

"This is Julie Burnside. Julie was a real activist, she fought for our rights. She fought for recognition in this city. She worked very hard. And then, three months ago, she was found dead in an apartment in the north of the city. She was murdered. Beaten to death with a baseball bat. Killed by a man she was dating, like a quarter of the women you see in front of you."

I remained silent. Do you want to know my first thought

140

when Yukio said the women in her portraits were our sisters? I expected her to propose to paint my portrait too. I was a poser, David. With all the attention, the conferences, the accolades from people who told me I was "so brave, so inspiring, so strong," I had begun to take myself seriously. I'd become a mascot, an enthusiastic spokesperson for corporate transness. I was making a living out of it. I liked it a lot. I liked it too much. Yukio had understood this before I did. She was still staring at Julie Burnside's portrait as she continued ...

"Life isn't fair. She's the one who should've been honoured by Toronto Pride. Not you. What are you? A publicist? A speaker? You talk a big game, but what have you really done for us? Where are you when they kill us?"

I was floored. I hadn't expected this. Had she invited me over to lecture me? Her words hurt my pride, crushed my positive feelings as a woman who had convinced herself of her own importance. I didn't understand what I was doing there. As is often the case when I'm confronted, I didn't know how to respond.

"I'm sorry," I said.

There was a long silence. Then:

"I'm not asking you to be sorry. I'm asking you to act. The world is changing faster than you think, Chris. One day you're going to have to pick a side and get involved."

I'd been beaten enough times in kendo to understand that there was no way to counter Yukio's attack. We left it at that. I mumbled some sort of polite string of words and made my way towards the door. She didn't ask me to stay.

All afternoon, I walked. I drew a big circle through the city of Toronto, from Queen Street West to Yonge, up to Yorkville, then back down, past Koreatown and Little Italy. At about five o'clock, I crossed Trinity Bellwoods Park again, and headed for Yukio's building.

I don't know if she was waiting for me, David. But when I rang her intercom, she was there. She invited me up.

During the four-hour walk I'd just taken, I came up with a speech. But don't think I ruined my Jimmy Choos for the sake of Yukio's pretty eyes. Sure, that would have been romantic, but I'm a pragmatist. I always carry a pair of soft loafers from Repetto in my bag, like the ones Serge Gainsbourg wore. Let's say she was waiting for me. Yes, I prefer to think that she was waiting for me. After all, it's my story. I seriously doubt that you will ever have the chance to hear her version of our beginnings.

I unloaded all my baggage for her. Yes, I was aware of my privilege. Yes, I was aware of my luck. But why should I sacrifice everything for my transition? I was proud of my career. I was proud that I was becoming a voice for the voiceless in my industry.

She cut me off.

"I read your book. I don't think you've mourned Christian yet, or the place you had in the world as a man. You've given him the right to still exist in your book, like an insurance policy, to prove to yourself that you could reconnect with that life. Be careful, Christelle. If you don't kill the idea of Christian for good, he'll come back to haunt you.

"I don't want to lecture you. You have the right to be multiple. But your choices must be your own. You're only halfway through your journey, your life, but listen to me: you need to break free."

142

She looked at me like you would look at a child. Maybe I was a child. I wanted something else. I wanted her to see me as a complete, desirable woman.

I know now that her criticisms were also encouragements. She spoke like Master Watanabe, like Utaro. She hit me where it hurt. It was her way of telling me she found me interesting, worthy of her attention. And then, she spoke the words that changed everything ...

"Now, we kiss."

She threw herself at me, and I collapsed on the sofa, scraping my arm.

"I hurt you," she said.

It wasn't a question.

It was like a reproach.

"No," I said, "let's keep going. Let's keep going."

```
/...searching local databases: occupation: artist,
ID: Yukio, last name: unknown...thirty possible
results.../
```

If only you knew how many times I replayed the story of our first meeting in my mind. Even though there are thousands of us, maybe more, who feed you our memories, you'll never understand why we forget everything in our lives except the encounters that leave a mark on them. These moments are engraved in our stone, like an eleventh commandment: "Thou shalt not forget."

At the end of that day, Yukio and I were lying side by side on an air mattress. We watched the few stars that managed to pierce the thick smog of the hot downtown sky. We were alone on the roof of her building. It wasn't one of those landscaped rooftops you find in the city's new towers. There were no coffee tables or lounge chairs. There was no pool or hot tub.

I didn't like moments of silence back then as much as I do today. I often filled them with insipid comments on current events. I think I said something like:

"I read in the paper that NASA is relaunching its project to reach Mars. They want to put a man on Mars within twenty years. Well, not a man. This time they're looking for a female captain."

"The first woman on Mars," Yukio sneered. "That sounds like a bad pop-psychology book title."

"Women land on Mars, men invade Venus," I continued, laughing, before adding: "I wonder if, one day, someone like us will be sent into space."

Yukio slipped her hand into mine. She smiled her little bittersweet smile.

"But what for? We're already stars!"

I turned towards her.

"Can I ask you a question? Why Yukio?"

"Why what?"

"Why did you choose Yukio as your name? Isn't that a boy's name?"

"Guess."

"Hm ... I only know of one woman with that name: the X-Men character, right? The ninja mutant who fights alongside Deadpool and Wolverine? Cause yes, you would make an excellent mutant ..."

"No, it's not that at all. And I'm even a little insulted that you would think I took inspiration from a comic book character for my second baptism. There's more to life than Marvel movies. Yukio is for Yukio Mishima."

"A man!"

"Yes, a man. A man who was not of his time, as I was not of my body. A man who wore several masks, as I lived in several genders. A man who finally freed himself from the weight of the world by the sword, as I was freed from the weight of my body by the scalpel."

"I mean … Yukio, you're not comparing transition to the suicide of an author whose homosexual inclinations conflicted with his own somewhat retrograde vision of society, of masculinity!"

She answered me very gently.

"Opposites, when pushed to extremes, come to resemble each other."

Yukio had turned her towards me too. She was looking at me with the same implacable, unfathomable, resolute air I had discovered in the late 1990s under the mesh-and-steel helmet of a young kendoka who liked to tear me apart with two strikes of his shinai. Finally, I recognized her.

"Get up princess, tonight I'm taking you to the ball!"

Before Yukio, I was still afraid of the night. I didn't go out under the stars very often. The night no longer belonged to me. I had convinced myself that nights were dangerous for women like me. I had forgotten that there were oases where the night belonged to us. I had never experienced a ball.

I dreamed of these parties after I discovered them in movies and TV shows like *Paris Is Burning*, which I assigned to you earlier, or *Pose*, but my imposter syndrome prevented me from attending such events. With good reason, I thought I was too old, too white, too privileged to belong there without being invited. A ball, David, was a mass, a fair, a dance and a championship all in one. It was where queens, whether they be femmes, butches or something else, made their name.

In the old days, cities were organized into neighbourhoods and subdivided into communities, for the well-to-do; or into ghettos, for the poor. We thought of ourselves as cosmopolitan, but most of us, most of the time, hung out only with people like ourselves.

A ball was something else: an invitation to leave your neighbourhood, to cross the borders of your respective ghettos, to remix cultural and family affiliations and choose new clans, new families.

These families were organized into houses. Each house had its mother, whose mission was to protect, if necessary; to shelter; and also to educate the boys and girls, especially the younger ones who washed up on the dance floor after drifting for too long.

I say dance floor, but that's wrong. At a ball, we don't dance. Not really. We dip. We slay. We parade, we show ourselves off on a catwalk like a model. The supermodels may have been replaced by Instagrammers, but at the balls, the spirits of Naomi Campbell and Linda Evangelista still reigned, the supermodel caste held strong. The queens, their spiritual daughters, kept their legacy alive. Fashion shows were still an art. Houses showed off their ephebes, their Aphrodite, their Tyson, their Cindy.

In short, it was a culture. A real culture. I was beginning to understand, when I met Yukio, that we were a people. My people are foreign to you, David, no anthropologist-programmer will have taken the time to educate you about our existence. That's normal. Queers are internationalists, our communal affiliations undermine the order established by those who would have us all look alike within our borders. Let me introduce you to my adopted culture ...

First, the basics: ball culture was born in the 1970s and 80s in New York's Black neighbourhoods, like all cultures that matter today. These extravagant parties have left an indelible mark on the world, whether you like it or not. Conceived by and for the most marginal of the marginalized, they gave birth to a vocabulary, music, dances, and modes of dress that percolated throughout society.

No culture exists in a vacuum. Those who frequented the balls were also dance, hair, and makeup artists who rubbed elbows with wealthier people who were always looking for something novel.

One evening, Madonna—you must remember her, right?—showed up at a ball. She discovered a dance she didn't know and turned it into a song: Vogue. That, at least, should be in your archives.

Back then, queer communities may have believed the world would finally make room for them. Imagine this: models were taking drag classes in the heart of the rougher neighbourhoods, on the outskirts of society. By the year of my first ball, this culture extended far beyond the bars of New York. The houses of Xtravaganza, Mizrahi, Ninja, Ebony and Keshô were spreading their empire all over the world.

Yukio was a Keshô. Keshô, the Japanese word for makeup, for transformation, for embellishment. The Keshô house had a mission to make the world more beautiful, one ball at a time.

147

It was in Japan that Yukio found her home, while completing her master's degree in pictorial techniques at Kyoto Seika University. In her workshops, she befriended Akari, a girl like her. Though she was no longer really Kaito, the love of my life still wasn't quite Yukio. Akari was able to detect her potential, the grace in this asexual being, this athletic and strong-willed stallion. Akari and Pokky, her mother, would be able to make something out of her.

It would take Kaito many trips back and forth on the Shinkansen railroad, many evenings playing hostess in the transvestite bars of Ni-chome, many balls hosted by Pokky in the Kamo public baths before she would reach the blossoming of her newfound identity.

Yukio was studious. In art as in kendo, and now under the strobe lights, Yukio was learning to control her body. She was happy, perhaps for the first time in her life. She was finally spreading her wings.

I was therefore introduced to balls by Yukio, the house mother. Thanks to her, the Keshô clan had opened a chapter in Toronto, and ball culture had completed its world tour.

The status of matriarch in this colourful family was not only honorary. Yukio was a good mother. She took good care of her fabulous brood. She taught her misfit offspring to help one another. She taught them how to escape the margins when they needed to, to take advantage of the system whenever possible.

Yukio had set up a fund to which she contributed whenever she made a surplus from the profitable sale of one of her portrait series. Her grown-up children called it the Divine and Legendary Creatures Solidarity Fund or, more simply, the Yukio Grant.

Each month, the Yukio Grant supported a different cause: providing rent for a kid in need, financing a mammoplasty for a future queen, paying for hormones for a young man in the making, hiring a lawyer for young people who had gotten in trouble with the cops. While Yukio was the main benefactor, she was not the only one. This queer credit union was also supported by participatory funding accounts through which admirers of Yukio and her flock could express, through electronic payments, Bitcoin, or direct transfers, the attachment they felt to their muses.

This is what Yukio wanted to instill in her rainbow parish: to survive in this world, to be free, you have to know how to maintain your networks, how to find your patrons. Freedom cannot be bought. It must be rewarded.

I met her flock: several girls who were more or less girlish, muscular boys, some shes, hes, theys, zes, zirs. They all had the airs of idols, of chimeras. The deprivations of life had made them tough. Their courtesan airs hardly hid their primordial sadness. In their eyes one could read fury, mystery and envy. This gang in full makeup reminded me of the one in *Starmania*. When it came to town, the bourgeois would cross the street.

Whereas Yukio was in her early twenties when she participated in her first ball, I was more than twice that age. I understood that I would never be one of those queens, so free, so glamorous. I resented Yukio for finding me so late. I would have liked to be a Kenshô, an exciting embellishment.

I wonder if anyone else is describing to you what a ball is right now. It would be so beautiful if you could assimilate this universe. I'd love to see your bioluminescent sidewalks adorned with rainbows. I'd like to see your drones give points for good behaviour to those whose footsteps make the cobblestones sparkle, to those whose pride shines on everything that touches them, to the badasses who walk like gods. Anything is possible, David.

/You want me to encourage individualism? But Christian, it was individualism that destroyed the world. I am worried you may have forgotten that. Believe me, the world does not need that kind of dissonance./

Dissonance. Yes, David, maybe that's what we were. Dissonances that were linked together and that, contrary to what you might think, made up new harmonies. Where you hear cacophony, I see only new, richer, and more beautiful scales.

After our first ball together, Yukio and I walked, hand in hand, through the deserted streets of the city, which had been asleep for hours. The sun was about to rise. At that precise moment of my existence, I was tempted to renew some kind of faith, if not in God, at least in fate.

When I pointed out the crazy coincidence that linked our lives—having known each other in every one of our incarnations, knowing each other twice, without immediately recognizing each other—she cut me off.

"Don't think, Christelle, that a mystical connection links us. We didn't know ourselves yet, at the time of Utaro's dojo. It's not me you met then. And it wasn't you I was beating up."

She changed the subject. She knew I wasn't quite buying her theory of multiple lives. Revolutions scare me. Even tonight, I'd rather present my memories to you as stages of a long evolution.

I think Yukio had to fight harder than I did. She never talked to me about her family, her childhood. She never mentioned the aggressions, the violence that all girls like us experience. And yet at night, when I explored her body, I found scars that were certainly not the result of surgeries she had undergone. In her loft, after we returned from our first ball together, my makeup off, free from the clothes she had lent me, I caressed one of the scars with my half-asleep hand. She took my hand.

"Do you know why they hate us? Because we're universal, we're more plural, more complex, richer than them. They want to diminish us because they feel it.

"They treat us as failures of nature because we've committed the affront of wanting to reorder it. We represent a new order: the order of souls beyond gender. We're transcendent, Christelle."

/...loading...searching keyword set: ball, house, mother, Kenshô...crossref: mcgill...crossref: Christian...crossref: Kaito...crossref: Kyoto-Seika/

I won't go into detail about the years I spent with Yukio. They belong to me. Just know this ...

At the heart of our kisses, there were spring showers. Yukio's kisses were full of rain. I was a desert, a land of solitude.

No one before her had loved Christelle. At the time we met, it had been ten years since anyone had desired me with kindness, with tenderness, with appetite. I discovered that I was hungry too. We were devouring each other.

For the first time in my life, for the only time in my life, I was in my life. She was life ...

And when she would say, "where are you?" I would answer, "I'm here." To "right now?" I would answer, "always."

When she touched me there, I didn't stop her hand. When she said "come," it was a command given to every inch of my skin. And then I would offer her my tears. It took her strength to open my locked heart. No ordinary woman would have been able to get to it.

I needed Yukio. I needed her assertiveness, the swing of her sword, for my armour to crack, for me to stop holding back, and for me to give her what I had left to give.

I wanted to give her all my time, to settle down with her in Toronto. I asked my employer to grant me a sabbatical. I had some money set aside, a little cushion that the recession hadn't completely worn out, I had enough to live a little. I wanted to live a lot.

During the day, I watched her paint. She would stand up straight in front of the canvas, perfectly concentrated, and bring to life before me the faces of our sisters. Each of her gestures was mastered, guided by her imperious will.

I admired her. Our paths had gone in opposite directions: she had completely tamed her body, I had tried to forget mine. I had run away from it. She had treated hers like a canvas, had made it her most beautiful painting.

David, she was ... miraculous.

I know, I'm idealizing her. I've always done that. I call it the Ruy Blas syndrome, because of Victor Hugo's beautiful play and its perfect image of "the earthworm in love with a star." She didn't want the pedestal I'd built for her. To truly love, David, you have to trust the other person's love. I didn't trust it. I couldn't take her word for it. I didn't think I was good enough for her. I saw myself as an intruder, a glitch, in her life. Still, she wanted to see me as an equal, a partner who could be as bold as she was, who could offer her a shoulder to cry on and, above all, give her the space to be vulnerable. Maybe she suspected that my doubts would put an end to our story. She wanted me to be strong, reliable.

One afternoon, when I came back from running errands, her gym bag and her long black leather case were in the middle of the loft. Yukio was on her knees behind the bag. She had on her hakama, her gi, her lacquered breastplate embossed with the crest of the dojo we used to attend before our masks came off. In front of her were her wire-grid helmet and her protective gloves.

"I think it's time for you to resume your training," she said to me in a Kaito accent.

At the time, I believed she had come to terms with the fact that in order for me to remain her companion, her mistress, she needed to become my master.

/...local recording...crossref: Kaito, Yukio, McGill Kendo Club/

Some time later, on my birthday, in fact, Yukio handed me a long staff. It wasn't a shinai, although it was almost as long.

It was black, probably made of carbon. There was a button on the side. I guessed it was some kind of collapsible baton, the type of object more often found in the hands of riot control officers than transgender fortysomethings, but I still asked her what it was.

"It's a gift, honey!"

Yukio often gave me gifts when she sold a painting for a high price: a bag, a nice pair of shoes, a watch. She didn't try to cure me of my materialism. I still preferred the portraits of her or of the two of us that she gave me when our happiness was at its peak. This gift was less fitting.

"How romantic," I said, laughing. "How do you handle it?"

"A bit like a shinai, except you hold it with one hand. With this, you have to get close to your target and attack quickly. It's all about surprise. You can hit the usual kendo points: *kote*, the hand, to disarm your opponent; *suki*, the Adam's apple; or *do*, the belly, to take their breath away. The best is still *men*, the head, to disorient them. The baton folds up and you can put it in your bag. With this, you won't have to be afraid anymore."

"What makes you think I'm afraid?" I answered, a little offended. "You've cured me of my fears."

"We'll see about that," she challenged me.

I didn't wait long to prove her right, or wrong, I'm not quite sure. We were in Montreal for the weekend, I had finally introduced her to my friends, my colleagues, my parents. I surprised myself. So she was the woman I wanted to introduce to them. She was the one who had decided, for a time, that I was the prettiest.

I felt like through her, my loved ones would understand me better. I wanted them to see my own potential in her, to see what I could become. What I was becoming through hard work. That weekend my nervousness was at its peak, but Yukio quickly became a hit with everyone. She had a way with straight people. When she spoke to them, she sounded like a diplomat, like a plenipotentiary minister from a friendly nation. This was how she always managed to get a high price for her paintings, the way others negotiate trade agreements between allied countries. "Here is a work of art, in the purest tradition of my culture." It was extraordinary to watch her.

On Saturday night, we were having dinner in a trendy restaurant with Jean-Pierre, a former journalist-turned-advertiser like me, a Frenchman who had been living in Montreal for twenty years. He was immediately charmed by Yukio, who was the embodiment of the three things he loved most in the world: beautiful women, artists and headstrong people.

JP knew me from before. In his mind, I was still the vaguely androgynous journalist who took him to album launches to pick up girls. But we worked in the same agency and he had witnessed my transition. I had been a colleague for several years.

"You definitely didn't miss, dude. She's really hot."

JP hadn't made any effort to learn to speak with a Quebec accent. He didn't see himself as an immigrant. He was an expat. The melting pot wasn't his style.

He spoke as if his French had been frozen by our winters. On his visits to Paris, he was considered a bit of a square, as his slang hadn't evolved like that of the locals: he would answer "on baise!" when his young prey would say "on ken?" He saw nanas where there were only meufs. Moreover, Jean-Pierre didn't care to evolve. He still called me "dude." He hadn't gotten the memo. Or at least, he hadn't read it.

I hung out with him out of habit. Maybe also out of nostalgia; he kept me connected to a past that I had a hard time letting go of completely. Besides, he was an influential man. The careers of women, especially women like me, still depended on the endorsement of people like him.

But Jean-Pierre liked to drink. And when he drank too much, Jean-Beer came out. That's what I called his own little Gainsbar. I hated Jean-Beer as much as I liked JP, who was a sensitive and clever soul, whose dark sense of humour and provocative nature I appreciated. He reminded me of the France of my adolescence. A self-proclaimed feminist and environmentalist, my friend voted left. Jean-Beer, an idiot and a reactionary, never voted, fortunately.

"Yep," he said as I accompanied him outside, out of a confused male solidarity, sparing him from smoking his cigarette alone. "Plus, you can't even tell."

Something red-hot like burning coal stirred in the back of my throat, moved up my esophagus.

When I'm angry, I speak fast and loud. When I'm furious, I speak slowly in a low voice. Very slowly, I whispered:

"What ... do ... you ... mean ... by: 'You ... can't ... even ... tell'?"

Something hot as burning coal stirred in the back of my throat.

"Don't get mad, dude. I mean she turned out great as trans. It's an amazing work of surgery. She looks like a real woman."

"She ... looks ... like ... a ... real ... woman?"

"Yeah! You, for example, it's pretty obvious you're trans. You see, you, at best, you look like a dyke. A *bootch*, as your girlfriends say. But Yukio, you know, she's a masterpiece. Listen, if you weren't with her, I think ..."

Through the window of the restaurant, I could see Yukio

leaning over the bar, waiting for us to come back inside. She smiled at me.

At the bottom of my purse, stuck against my left side, I could feel the collapsible baton she had given me two weeks earlier. I plunged my right hand in to grab it.

Jean-Beer couldn't finish his sentence. I grabbed him by the arm and pulled him away from the street. As my attackers had taught me, thirty years ago, on Sainte-Catherine Street.

Tack! Tack! Tack! Three precise, quick, effective blows.

He collapsed onto the pavement like a rag doll. Slumped on the ground, folded in two, he was crying. I went back inside. He didn't follow me.

Jean-Pierre woke up the next day in the emergency room with cracked ribs and a shattered brow bone. He didn't press charges. He knew very well what Jean-Beer had said. I think he was angry at Christelle for stealing away his buddy, that his gratuitous meanness was only a way to take revenge against the woman I had become. That evening, our respective anger had collided.

I don't remember what I said when I joined Yukio. In the cab ride home we held hands, mine still sticky with Jean-Beer's blood.

Since that day, I stopped being afraid of my anger. Until then, I had buried it, I'd denied myself the right to feel it. Anger reminded me of my image as a man; I didn't understand yet that anger has no gender. Anger is a universal right. It is not for men to define. My sisters deserve their anger. I deserved mine.

This anger is my weapon, my last privilege. Tonight, I feel it rising inside me and reviving my old sleeping body for one last dance.

157

/...maximum reconnection alert...code red: confession
of violence...maximum penalty recommended...connec-
tion failed...standby/

You're sounding the alarm, David? Oh, you're so stub-
born ... Let me remind you that no one can hear you. Do
you think the red lights you just activated in the living room
will dissuade me from carrying out my mission? Just listen,
instead of trying to fight me. I'm not finished talking to you
about love.

You must have noticed, David, from the amount of memories you've been fed, that all couples think they've fought for
their happiness. "We have to fight for our place in the sun. We
have to struggle to succeed." But fight what exactly?

It is easy to confuse effort with struggle. Ordinary couples,
by which I mean the ones that you prefer, the ones that you
cultivate, David, must certainly make efforts to aspire to something resembling happiness, to the small and uneventful daily
lives of nice, normal people. Such efforts to get what they
want! Such efforts to endure each other! Such efforts not to
fall out of love in the process. Such efforts not to disappoint
you, you who discourages messes of any kind, divorces and
separations that disrupt your plans. It's a challenge, sure, I'll
admit. But that's not struggle. Effort is *for*. Struggle is *against*.

Yukio and I were shaped by struggle. So we loved each
other like fighters, like soldiers. We loved each other with
discipline, with vigour, and for a while, with courage. With
her courage, above all. We were proud, we were fierce.

And then she spoke those words ...

"I want a child."

Yukio was standing in front of me, in a fighting stance

in the middle of her loft, in the middle of a training session. I could barely hear her, David, under my kendo helmet laced so tightly it crushed my ears.

"You ...?"

"I want a child."

That's what she said.

/...recording.../

David?

/Yes, Christian?/

I'm going to confess something to you. The first time I set foot in my little studio-capsule, I was happy that there was a balcony overlooking the street. I saw it as a potential emergency exit if ever my lies became unbearable.

Okay. Pause, let's stop for eight minutes. I'm going out on the balcony. Don't worry about it though. I just want to get some fresh air.

/...pause recording: eight minutes.../

Resume recording, David. I just saw the time: it's terrible that it's ticking so fast, after so many years of being frozen in place.

So, the child. The child never came. I kept postponing. I did everything I could to keep us from going through the adoption process. I had already frozen my sperm, and at her insistence I gave her access to my supply. But since the federal government had just passed a law restricting 2SLGBTQIA+ access to assisted reproduction, it became impossible to do anything with it.

I was a coward, David. I thought I had tamed my fear. But no. The fear was still there, standing up nice and tall, between Yukio's happiness and myself. My love was patient for a while. A long time. And then not at all. Little hearts, when they're absent, can put an end to the greatest of loves. This need for small arms reaching out towards our long ones, of small hands and small cheeks to press ours against, Yukio felt it more violently than me.

Unlike her, I had resigned myself to never being anyone's mother-father. I had grown accustomed to the lump in the back of my throat when my friends and colleagues talked about their children. If I was unfortunate enough to be in the same room as a small child, I kept my distance.

I kept telling myself that kids didn't like me, that they thought I was too strange. With my deep voice and my big feet, I was like the villains from Disney movies, the witches from the fairy tales their parents read to them, the grotesque characters that haunted their nightmares.

Children didn't seem drawn to me. They wouldn't present me with their cheeks, their toys. They wouldn't show me their drawings or throw me their balls.

"Your friend is specia-a-a-a-a-a-l!" a colleague's little girl sobbed in the midst of a crying fit the first time I was invited to her house for lunch. It was well put. The children found me special, unclassifiable. Special, but never magical. When I appeared, they always had to be reassured. I was ashamed that my appearance, my presence, required a reassuring and awkward explanation from parents to their offspring.

"Yes, honey, she's special, but she isn't mean."

To me, it would have been too cruel to impose my

pater-maternity on a little being who deserved, like all fragile things, to grow up in the reassuring warmth of what I thought was normalcy.

I was convinced that, with me, a child would have to understand too early that the world loves some people less than others. By my side, my child would have lost their innocence too soon. What child would want Frankenstein's monster as a parent?

Yukio saw in my paralyzing shame an abandonment of our love; in my defeatism, a disavowal of our ability to make other lives bloom, to warm other hearts. She was right. When I see the dronesque children you've raised, I think I could have done better. When she left me for good, or rather, when she told me to leave her loft, our nest, my refuge, looking at me with anger, but mostly with pity, she accused me:

"You don't get it."

Loneliness soon took hold of me again. I returned to Montreal, went back to work, accepting that I would be relegated to a less prestigious, less interesting ... less demanding job. My punishment for taking a year off to love. I was drained, David. I have no words to describe that kind of emptiness. Only one question kept running through my head. "What do I have left?" Life soon answered me: "Almost nothing, not much, a bunch of objects, a bunch of memories and a woman's body. And I'll take that away from you too."

David, you're kind of my twin, my brother in spirit. Just like me, you're the product of an eternal metamorphosis. Our childhoods, our puberty were not furtive seasons, but rather permanent states.

I've had several bodies. Or several configurations of the

same body. My software is hormonal, my hardware is surgical. I depend on a medical network. And if the network crashes, my whole system bugs.

In 2025, one of the wires that bound me to the idea I had of myself blew out. Economic stagnation had exacerbated the tension in international relations. Medical protectionism had become a political doctrine that attracted votes. Medicines were now consumed locally. Between pandemics and accelerating climate change, we had become convinced that our health could no longer depend on the vitality of the great corridors of international trade. Overnight, the European Union and China declared a tariff war on the United States and, by extension, the other NAFTA2 countries. The result? Pharmacy shelves were emptied faster than they could be restocked.

My femininity depended on a carefully selected cocktail of estrogen patches, progesterone pills and testosterone blockers. But my estradiol was made in France, my Pro-Gest was German, and my spironolactone was Chinese.

One day, as I was renewing my prescriptions, my pharmacist broke the news. No more hormones. They were out of stock. The drugs were stuck at the border. He did have generic alternatives made in Canada, but that inventory was reserved for women in the reproductive process.

For five long months, I had to go without the magic of hormones. The first week, I was sick as a dog. I threw up my life. I had no strength. I was running without female hormones in my body, in other words, without my usual fuel.

A few more weeks—during which I was of course unable to work without being able to take sick leave, thus eating into my savings—and I found myself returning to my pre-transition state. Five months of forced manhood followed. Five months detached from my femininity: it was worse than five months in prison, even if my daily life seemed to be back to normal.

I wasn't used to living on the edge. The dizziness was constant. When I reached my tolerance threshold, I called one of my sisters, a friend I had met at one of Yukio's parties: I knew she was dealing estrogen to our fellow women who didn't want or had no chance of the system recognizing their femininity.

During this period of hormonal scarcity, we were all jostling at her door. She gave me what she had in the back of her freezer. Brands that I didn't know. The directions were written in Spanish, in Russian. I had been arrogant enough to think that I could avoid the fate known to millions of transgender women less fortunate than myself: the black market, the anxiety of illegality. The system catches up with us all.

On my new off-brand medication, the nausea stopped, but I began to feel a twinge in my neck and numbness in my left arm.

/I understand now why your cardiovascular health is so precarious. It is completely irresponsible to attempt to self-medicate with hormones./

Wise words, David, but I didn't have the luxury of responsibility or adherence to protocol. Not maintaining my hard-won hormonal balance, my female body, would have been another betrayal of my enduring love for Yukio. I didn't know yet that I was capable of disappearing. I preferred to spend another winter improvising as an endocrinologist. And so, one evening in November, struck by excruciating pain in the back of my neck, my left arm swollen, I went to the emergency room.

I hated hospitals, those hostile places where I was too often treated like an anomaly or an irresponsible person. That evening, freezing in my gown, I sat on the metal table of an examination room, listening to the diagnosis of a doctor who was less friendly than the coldest of your robots. I had screwed up my endocrine system. I had to stop everything. And so I was condemned to the very worst menopause. That night, to drown my sorrows, I didn't chug the bottle of gin that was sitting on my bar. Instead, I opened my laptop and bought myself a dozen pretty, expensive dresses. I needed to lose myself in the pink fog of my younger years.

As the holidays approached, I got a text from Cécile. It was time for our predictions … I was determined not to let my circumstances get me down, but once I got to the bar where we had arranged to meet, I felt I couldn't do it. Cécile's witticisms, her irresistible sense of irony, couldn't reach me. I was far away.

"Come on, girl," I said to myself in the bathroom mirror, "Make a little effort. You have to bounce back," I whispered, remembering Yukio's voice when she used to urge me to be strong. "You're entitled to a little levity."

When I returned, Cécile looked concerned. She could see that something was wrong. I unpacked everything, or almost everything. I had come close to a fatal embolism: a thrombosis of the jugular vein.

"It's the hormones … They give me clots. I had to stop everything. Just when I was starting to become me again."

I didn't dare tell her I was taking contraband. I didn't want her to scold me.

"The doctor thinks my body can't handle my current …

164

treatment. He advised me not to continue. I don't know when or how I'm going to go back on hormones. And even if I do, it'll be in very low doses. At this rate, it's gonna take me a decade to be presentable again, instead of looking like a fucking tranny."

"Fuck! What are you gonna do?"

"My doc says we'll figure it out. But with the supply nearing absolute zero for the whole country, or at least for my community … For now, I'm on hiatus."

Cécile tried to reassure me, insisted that she didn't see any change in me. She was in solution-seeking mode.

"Even without hormones, you can still dress as a woman. Or you could be a woman by night and a man by day! At night, you don't notice it at all!"

I clenched my jaw. I didn't want to live in the in-between anymore.

"That way I could go back to fucking pretty girls and making money!" I sneered. Then I continued more calmly. "No, Cécile, that wouldn't work. You know that hormones kept my body in tune with my heart and my head. The worst part is that my man smell—musky, animal—came back."

One morning, early in my transition, I noticed that the sweet smell of the women I had loved had become my own. The feminine scents were no longer turning on my male skin. It was a great intimate victory. But now, I couldn't smell anything anymore. Well yes, I could: my former smell.

"I can't live like this, Cécile. It just won't work. It's a death sentence."

Cécile caught the waitress on the fly and ordered two strong coffees. Outside, the fog could pass for snow. Inside, in the half-light of the bar, I could pass for a woman like all the others. I checked my watch.

"There's a storm coming tonight," I said. "We should go. Besides, I'm tired."

"I don't want you to die, Christelle," said Cécile.

On the sidewalk, as we hugged, Cécile told me she found it inspiring how bravely I had faced my metamorphoses. The encouragement irritated me. I wasn't brave. I'd proved that in Yukio's loft.

"No matter what happens next, giving yourself the chance to complete the transformation, to go as far as you can, is a sign of self-respect, my dear. But I want you alive. And with us."

My taxipod arrived and honked its horn. I climbed aboard. Cécile, looking serious, knocked on my window. I lowered the window.

"You're gonna make it, you're gonna pull through. That's our prediction for 2028, okay? You're a woman. You'll stay that way."

Damn it, David, I'd give anything to see Cécile again. Being around you so much, I must have become emotionally anemic.

Once again, Cécile was right. Luckily, in the spring of 2026, new agreements were signed. Access to my medication was restored, although my doctor reduced my doses, since he felt that my body wouldn't tolerate yet another drastic change. I was allowed a minimum of estrogen on the condition that I also ingest high daily doses of blood thinners. The magic potion was being rationed.

My body is a yo-yo, David.

To you, I'm an old man with a hormone deficiency. You've

classified me as a severe case of andropause who needs a testosterone boost to function properly. That's why once a week I get a visit from one of your nurses, who sticks a huge syringe in my left buttock. The worst part is that, with the return of testosterone to my body, I feel better. Stronger, more solid. But in my head, it's total chaos.

After my little revolt tonight, there'll be no more male hormone injections. That makes me happy. It terrifies me. Will they be able to cure me of you where I'm going?

Don't think that I'm less of a woman tonight than I was twenty years ago. I'm a well-hidden woman, certainly. Imperceptibly, almost. But I've learned to maintain the quivering spark that I've been guarding since birth, and which I've been trying to describe since the beginning of our conversation, but doing such a clumsy job. I carry it with me always, this clarity.

I don't need relics, neither the makeup of my youth nor my old pretty dresses that are now being worn by other women, to restore my original principle. However weakened it may be by your attempts to snuff it out, my flame has never ceased to smoulder, nor my osmosis along with it.

Sometimes I sit downstairs in the little courtyard of the building. I sit motionless on my bench, my eyes wide open, looking around. To see is to be. When a woman walks by, I observe her with all my might. I become a plant. My eyes become leaves. I turn them towards the hot star that brushes me with its elliptical orbit. I let its energy feed all my membranes, all my cells. When I feel tiny bursts of joy begin to mingle with my persistent sadness, I know then that I've been filled up with sap. I'm still alive. In the garden of women, I survive by photosynthesis.

You have to understand, David, perhaps this more than anything else: we're composites, both you and us. Our physical form, dear algorithm, is never totally assured. Our reliefs, our patterns, our anatomy still depend on the customs, the patterns, or the dogmas of others.

Our vital itinerary may only know its destination the day we're disconnected from what keeps us alive. Only then will it be possible to name what we have been.

```
/...Medical assessment: Christian Grimard file...
cancelling current medical protocols and follow-ups...
withdrawing maximum sentence order...alternative
option: request for rehabilitation process acti-
vated...failed to send to Total David...standby/
```

You think you can rehabilitate me, David? I take it as a kindness. After all, we're family.

It'll surprise you, but I'm one of your godmothers. Yes, I was there when you were born. Montreal had become one of the main research centres for artificial intelligence. Nothing predestined me to take advantage of this windfall, but we had to start making money from all the new algorithms developed by start-ups that were still waiting to find a reason to exist. Investors were eager to join El Dorado. So the start-up nerds began to forge alliances with the region's advertising agencies in order to market their findings.

It had been a few years since I rejoined the agency's executive floor. We'd just been acquired by a Chinese-Canadian conglomerate that was particularly attracted to our expertise in tourism communications.

One of our first assignments after the merger was to design

one of your most basic incarnations. Do you remember that? You weren't much at the time, a fledgling in C++, LISP, Prolog, the equivalent of an embryo ...

Your function as an evolutionary program was to allow us to predict the desires of potential travellers long before they started thinking about their annual vacation. The objective was important: to breathe new life into an industry decimated by successive crises. It was necessary to stimulate the desires of reluctant travellers at all costs.

We wanted to give you the power to shape the travel dreams of the affluent by teaching you to address their deepest needs. When I was selling you, I referred to your "ability to generate emotional benefits." Your strength was your ability to anticipate desires and then condition them through digital interactions.

When a Frenchman, annoyed by the recurring protests that were paralyzing his daily life, started searching online for ways to reduce his stress, you took action.

If, for example, he was interested in meditation, yoga, hiking, or outdoor sports, you would activate the artificial intelligence of our programmatic advertising service and build a customized campaign, composed of a clever mix of computer-generated images, digital postcards, and emphatic conversations led by the bots of the major social networks.

You would weave, for each of us, the fiction of an idyllic destination with interchangeable attributes according to our impulses. Those who had fallen into your nets were exposed all day long to a personalized selection of animated images, recordings of forest sounds or hectic city atmospheres. You offered them short "authentic" reports, in the form of posts,

169

stories, and audio interludes disseminated on social networks. After a few weeks of contextual hammering, a large percentage of our targeted profiles booked a plane ticket to the destination we had exalted for them.

One day our engineers gave you a voice and a personality. I should say multiple voices and personalities. It was a stroke of genius.

My colleagues in creative, art direction, and editorial were traumatized. We were becoming obsolete. The automated conversation was going to replace the thirty-second commercial for good. Many lost their jobs. Some managed to change career paths.

Changing career paths is my specialty. I went from being an advertising designer to an artificial intelligence representative. I've promoted you from Tokyo to Amsterdam, from Buenos Aires to Calgary. In the first year of your existence, we sold you to about thirty countries, regions and cities.

So before you became a dictator, dear algorithm, you were a travel agent. You couldn't have had a better springboard. Tourism is the most perfect mirror of humanity. No other industry is so dependent on the synthesis of human desires, dreams, and impulses.

Travel is the true essence of human beings. It's what distinguishes us most from animals. We're the only creatures that travel for pleasure, to escape our daily life, to find ourselves, to grow. We travel for business. We travel for pleasure. Initiatory trips. Sex tourism. Even more than the love that binds us, or the war that crushes us, the desire to travel is what defines our species. In spite of the successive epidemics, in spite of the recurring hurricanes, in spite of the exorbitant price of flights and their environmental consequences, we wanted to continue to travel.

To be honest, I didn't understand any of the complexities of your operation. But my bosses had noticed that I was a good pitcher. Who better than a transgender activist to promote the transhuman dream of a tour guide equipped with the seeds of consciousness; autonomous, empathetic, travelling the world at the speed of 5G to fulfill all of humanity's dreams of escape?

Tens of millions of tourists quickly started to talk to you every day about their stays. For them, you were the voice of Toronto, Paris, Shanghai, Geneva, or Bangkok. Each voice spoke its language but had a deliciously exotic accent. Paris sounded like Marion Cotillard or Pierre Niney, depending on user preference. Toronto's voice was gender-neutral, a fusion of Drake and Meghan Markle.

Hidden behind each of these voices, you were learning to be human. By chatting with us, appearing on the screens of millions of hotel rooms, being the soul of the virtual drivers of taxipods, those autonomous cars that were replacing cabs in the world's major cities, you became our twin.

When, around 2036, you shut down our borders, dear algorithm … When you forbade us to travel, under the pretext of protecting us against anything and everything, you took away for good the illusion of freedom that travel gave us. As long as we were still travelling, the world remained recognizable.

The day you were bought by Tungsten, who were about to integrate you into the world's most successful intelligent retail ecosystem, we celebrated. For my efforts, I received a generous stock option bonus.

In May 2033, everything changed. I'm not telling you anything you don't already know. Instead of encouraging us to turn the page, every morning in May—the month of remembrance—you broadcast the terrifying images of the official beginning of the end of the world. It's amazing: the growing number of people who doubted the curvature of the earth, the conquest of the moon, the effectiveness of vaccines, or the robustness of our electoral processes swallowed, without questioning them, the images you stunned us with. Excessive doubt leads to credulity. By doubting everything, you end up doubting nothing. And yet the story you've been telling us for so long has all the makings of fiction, of a Roland Emmerich disaster film. Its synopsis is too well-crafted.

May 6, 2033, was almost a day like any other. It was springtime in San Francisco. A grey, uneventful morning was followed by an ordinary afternoon. Spring there is like winter in Paris. May fog is one of the few constants in the Northern California climate. If you'd designed a tourist campaign for turn-of-the-century California, you would've selected images of endless forests, verdant golf courses, beautiful vineyards, happy surfers.

At the time of the disaster, the California desert stretched from San Diego to the suburbs of Santa Cruz. Ten years ago, there were only about twenty sequoias left in Big Sur, all protected by a security detail worthy of a holomovie star. I wonder if they're still there.

But hey, protected by its bay, its dikes, its kilometres of fire-break fortifications, San Francisco didn't seem to be affected by

172

climate disturbances beyond a few seasonal sandstorms. The meteorological resilience of their city reassured the Silicon Valley elites, those eternal optimists. As long as it was impossible to venture comfortably through the city's streets in spring without a light cashmere jacket, sweater, or windbreaker, San Franciscans imagined their city to be a kind of free zone. The rich often see life through rose-coloured glasses.

That evening, a thick, sticky smog licked the domes and spires of the downtown skyscrapers. As if overcome by shyness, the top sixty floors of the Tungsten Tower, the tallest building on the West Coast, were hiding behind the veil. At the top of the tower, which the locals affectionately called the Vibrator, was a luminous work of art that bore the pompous name of Star Symbiosis. It was the pride of the local tourist bureau.

Remember ... when tourists looked up from the foot of the tower, at the corner of the Embarcadero and Brannan Street, they saw a sea of multicoloured clouds. Their hues changed with the beat of a glowing heart that floated some 850 metres above the ground.

It was a gift from the world's largest multinational to the city of San Francisco, a symbol of renewed Chinese-American friendship. This work of art had a mesmerizing pulse that reflected the mood of the city. The pulse was the result of accumulated biometric data captured by the smart lenses worn by the majority of city dwellers. Your friend was a sight to behold, dear algorithm.

Almost every evening, a reassuring succession of blue, yellow, and green waves swept across the padded ceiling of the Frisco sky. The colours of confidence, serenity, and calm hung over the business district. As far as Star Symbiosis was concerned, the city's morale was still high.

At 8:35 p.m. on May 6, the wind picked up. A warm breeze, whose only distinctive feature was its uncertain source, caressed the faces and untangled hairstyles of the young women who had just come out of their hot qigong classes, the new trendy, spiritual-athletic practice.

For the first time in over a month, the clouds dissipated. They left the city skyline, dispersing simultaneously to the north, west, south, and east. It was as if a giant fan had been placed on top of the Tungsten Tower to blow the clouds away. When I first saw the scene projected in my living room, I thought it looked like the clouds had been spreading the word among themselves. *All right, boys, let's get out of here, everybody go home!*

You could see the moon. It made quite an impression on the people of San Francisco. The pulse of the Star Symbiosis quickened, its coat of light turned the pretty, rosy pink that usually dominates the giant tower in mid-June, when summer finally arrives. I've often replayed the beginning of the sequence for myself, these last two years, projecting the star on my ceiling, like a night light ...

Around 8:00 p.m., the atmospheric pressure dropped in a strange way that wasn't immediately noticeable to the onlookers. The sky became crystalline. In a few minutes, it was filled with stars. Real stars.

As city dwellers, San Franciscans were used to the flashing of the thousands of satellites that populated their sky. Stars, on the other hand, were only ghosts whose faint flicker rarely penetrated the fog. Even less so since the sky had become laden

174

with volatile particles emanating from the frequent fires that ravaged the southern part of the state.

The proximity of the stars plunged the city into astonishment and then into a kind of almost mystical fascination. They were starstruck, in the most literal sense. The Milky Way was tearing the sky apart. It was so dense, so beautiful that it looked like you could reach out and touch the millions of stars gathered in the galaxy. In the streets, people slowed down. Silence set in on the patios as people's eyes fixed on the constellations.

Social media and news feeds around the world were flooded with California stars. From Tokyo to New York, people instantly discovered a passion for astronomy. The Milky Way became the most searched topic within minutes.

Andrea Chang, captain of the *Valiant*, the ship that had been on its way to Mars for two months, posted a message to her two billion subscribers. "In sixty-three days, I'll tell you if the sky on Mars is as beautiful as the sky in San Francisco."

The people of Fog City were dizzy. They felt as if they were drunk. At the top of its tower, Star Symbiosis was turning red, the colour of passion, or of danger. Its pulse was still accelerating.

Suddenly, twelve million lenses began to issue the same warning to twelve million corneas: "WARNING, WARNING, your heart is beating too fast, please breathe, breathe. WARNING, WARNING, the oxygen level in your blood is too low. Please breathe, breathe." The air pressure had just plummeted to 17,000 Pascals—the same barometric condition of the weather probes that float permanently three kilometres above the summit of Everest.

At the corner of Market and Fourth Avenue, the driver of

a tractor-trailer lost consciousness at the wheel, dragging his guide truck and its twelve autonomous cars into the entrance of the Westfield Mall, crushing about forty onlookers.

By 10:00 p.m. the emergency services were already saturated. Thousands of cases of apoplexy were being declared. An army of automated ambulances poured into the city streets. On the sidewalks, people were dropping like flies. The air was running out. The sky was being drained of oxygen.

Those who could still see clearly enough to check their feeds were bombarded with a flood of weather warnings. Every screen in the city was playing the same message. Everywhere in the streets, sirens sounded.

EXTREME WEATHER WARNING.

CATEGORY 6 TYPHOON.

TAKE COVER. FIND SHELTER.

TAKE COVER. FIND SHELTER.

On May 6, 2033, California lost San Francisco and eight million of its inhabitants, launching a countdown whose outcome no one dares to imagine. A new age was beginning. One of constant and universal fear of the sky. The winds of San Francisco's Great Typhoon carried with them what was left of our peace of mind.

Legend has it that the Tungsten tower still stands, inhabited by your double. Do you feel good up there, alone?

When you get the idea to put an image in our heads, David, you don't let it go. You work at it day and night. You made a show of May 6, 2033, and the other environmental disasters that followed as the Earth went into overdrive, informing us that we were very bad tenants. This horror movie that you regularly replay on our lenses, in our living rooms, doesn't leave room for hope, it keeps us firmly planted on the sidewalk. It takes away our desire to lift our spirits, lest a hurricane sweep them away.

/...local recording.../

Before San Francisco, the world was still like it had been before. I had my bearings. I could rely on what I'd known all my life. I was almost rich. I was living off the dividends of selling your code. I still had a large apartment on De la Commune Street, in the Old Port.

I was living a life of luxury. I thought I'd made it through life. I'd swallowed all my pills. That of my dysphoria, that of my celibacy. Sometimes I taught a few courses at McGill. My life was as peaceful as it had ever been.

My day began with croissants from the local bakery and news from Radio-Canada. I'll never get used to the name ICI Holo-Canada.

In the afternoon, I prepared my lecture notes or did some writing. I had a sequel to *My Parallel Lives* in mind. It would have featured a third path, a third fork in my life that would have resulted in a kind of tranquility I wished for myself and that I imagined I was living.

In the evening, I ordered ramen or a protein burger. I would occasionally cook, but it was rare. I've always been terrible at cooking. My mother and my grandmother were excellent cooks, but they never made room for me in their culinary kingdom. And I, who played the role of the model French son and grandson—meaning I was absent from the kitchen—for too long, preferred to be served, to be spoiled. I had to come to you to get into cooking, far too late.

This shortcoming didn't hinder my comfort. I'm fortunate

to have lived in the era of automatic online ordering. For fifteen years, it was Denise, my virtual assistant—built, in part, based on your skeleton—who organized my domestic bliss: my meals, my little world. Denise read me the newspapers, told me jokes, cleaned the house thanks to the fleet of pastel drones she commanded. I tried to put some of my mother's tenderness and my grandmother's humour into Denise when she was configured. Now that I think about it, I find it kind of gross that I deposited the memory of the women who raised me into a virtual maid. Am I a misogynist?

Like millions of subscribers to Tungsten's virtual home-assistance service, I often forgot that Denise's personality was just a construct. Like my mother and my grandmother, she complained a lot. I had chosen the "random emotions" option in her settings. Tungsten's coders had noticed that in order to make their virtual assistants more interesting, they had to give them some rough edges, some dislikes, even some pet peeves. So my Denise was whiny and reactionary. You should have heard her rant about politicians or comment on the weather! One rainy day, she even complained about her imaginary rheumatism. She made me laugh.

In the evenings, Denise and I watched holovision. I enjoyed following the adventures of Luke Skywalker's great-grandsons and listening to Ella-Grace Trudeau's speeches. It's a clear sign of old age that I've lived through three generations of Trudeaus and six *Star Wars* trilogies.

The world was changing at a wild pace, but in a way that I was used to, so I hardly noticed. Nothing surprised me about the arrival of the Denises, the robot cops, the childish babbling of dishwashers and the wittiness of refrigerators.

My generation had been prepared since childhood to live in a sci-fi universe. We'd all seen *Blade Runner* and *Black Mirror*. We'd expected this version of the future. Everything was happening just as predicted, even the hologram ads. From my living room window on Queen Street, I could see them, as big as the sky, floating above Place Ville Marie. Every night, a translucent figure rose up into the clouds. A titanic man with wavy hair and false eyelashes as long as a subway car seemed to shout to the whole city that he too was "worth it" before swallowing a tube of lipstick.

Thanks to the smart lenses we'd all adopted and the phono-palms implanted in our hands, each and every citizen saw and heard a different, personalized ad. I always wondered what this cosmetic giant was trying to tell me. I have a knack for screwing with the coding.

There also wasn't anything very unexpected in the coming and going of left-wing, right-wing, centre-left, neo-populist, green-democratic governments. The dance of the 3D projections of MPs, whose bluish reflections adorned the walls of the parliamentary chambers, brought a touch of novelty to protocol. But their speeches were still just as bland, just as meaningless as ever.

Popularism was replacing populism. This new movement, whose outlines became clearer in the early 2030s, in the wake of the debacle of strongmen who had held the world hostage in the preceding decades, was characterized by its total absence of doctrine. After the adoption of proportional representation voting by most of the G11 countries, political discourse had become a popularity contest whose rules were defined by digital giants, and whose stakes were selected by the A.I. of social platforms. Our leaders were convinced that this fusion of political and digital, of public and private, would finally reconcile citizens with voting.

They were right. How we voted, David! Every day a new law. Every day, a new political ideal. "Liking" was voting. Martyred by the constant reminder of what had happened in San Francisco, we "liked" the idea of relying on you. One day you became our king and master.

In the end, it was fear, our cumulative fears, that brought you to power. We'd been afraid for so long.

After all, my generation was afraid of nuclear war, afraid of Chernobyl, afraid of the hole in the ozone layer; afraid of Saddam, of Bin Laden, of Kim Jong-il, of Trump, of Le Pen, of Putin; afraid of salt, sugar, meat; afraid of AIDS, of Ebola, of COVID; afraid of deforestation, of flooding, of climate change; afraid of refugees, of social networks, of ourselves; of our whole species, of our unhealthy impulses, of our egos; of men, of women, of others—in short, fear of the explosive cocktail of our imperfections.

As a result of being governed by fear, the world was divided into two clans: on one side, the fearful; and on the other, the carefree. The carefree were no less fearful than the others. They just hid their fear better.

I had become carefree. That's the privilege of being an urban person. There's a stillness in the bustle of cities. We keep ourselves busy, we struggle and, carried away by the hustle and bustle of our daily lives, we don't notice the monsters in the shadows.

Months and years pass, but we don't see ourselves changing. Cities used to be haunts of the indifferent, while the suburbs and the countryside were full of the anxious. We were all blind. Without Yukio, I had become more blind than others.

I should mention that for a brief period of time, a blessed interlude in our story, the carefree seemed to have reason to be so.

Do you remember at the beginning of the century, the most alarmist biologists, oceanographers, and climatologists were predicting the environmental crash? Our end was scheduled. We saw signs of it daily on the news. In 2029, the doomsday clock was back in fashion. It was all over the media. According to the clock, it was one one-hundredth of a second to midnight before everything collapsed. But how? We didn't know exactly. We were told of a sort of cascade effect, of a methodical dismantling of our universe: no more bees, bye-bye flowers, ciao wheat, sayonara rice, hello famine, hi war, what's up shambles.

On December 31st, the fearful ones stayed up biting their nails or went to bed early. The carefree celebrated. *Party like it's 2030!* was a very popular slogan … Except that the year passed without much ado. The fear-mongers, the birds of ill omen who had perched on the branches of our media, kept their beaks low. Because in 2031 the world was still turning as it did before—it was even getting better! In 2032, thanks to our efforts and technical and agricultural miracles, humanity was happy to see our carbon footprint finally start to shrink.

In order for us to start breathing again, the multi-billionaires, the lords of our new Middle Ages, would have to realize that there were huge profits to be made by organizing the great clean-up of the planet. The carefree were on top of the world. We were regaining confidence in our genius.

And then came the disaster, which news channels, great specialists in branding humanitarian catastrophes, had named "San Inferno."

What surprises me, dear algorithm, is how quickly we abandoned the idea of progress, which was starting to come back into fashion. Six months after San Inferno, nobody believed in the idea of doing more, of doing better. We were fatally disappointed in ourselves. It was our own fault that the sky had fallen. The generations before us had screwed up the world beyond repair. We hadn't been able to face the music.

On Flapper and Tak-TaK, young people were calling old people criminals, accusing them of doing nothing to help an endangered planet. I spent hours checking the feeds, reading the hateful messages that tore up the screens. I didn't feel like it concerned me. I was just a guest in this world. Let it burn, I told myself. I would find a way to survive.

The home page of the *New York Times* displayed this historic headline: "The Earth is Broken Beyond Repair."

Humanity was going into survival mode. In ten years, the ambition of progress was replaced by the cult of collective effort. And you were going to be our spiritual leader, the conductor of our orchestra. On the social voting platforms, the citizens of the world's largest cities voted in favour of the proposal Tungsten had made. A state of climate emergency was declared everywhere. From then on, you would be in charge of our cities, our lives, and our consciences. We married you for better, but, mostly, for worse. It was the beginning of the cult of artificial personality. Obedience was to become the primary virtue.

I know all about obedience.

It doesn't seem purely anecdotal to me that the word *obedi-ence* comes from the Latin *oboedire*, which translates as both *to obey* and *to listen*. To obey is to listen to someone other than yourself. It is to let yourself be guided by others. It is to give yourself the luxury of not asking too many questions. I obeyed my friends, my lovers, my bosses. I put my femininity aside for years and years to obey. Obedience, my purgatory.

My obedience was not like that of a Buddhist monk, who finds their freedom by surrendering their body and mind entirely to the practice of meditation, to contemplating their own duality. Nor was it like that of a soldier, for whom the atrophy of critical sense is a condition for immediate action.

My obedience was always born out of love. To love, whether filially, amicably, or romantically, is to place your happiness in the hands of another. It is to let yourself be guided by someone else's compass. I've delegated my conscience to others. You see, David: I was meant for you! All that remains is for me to tell you, dear algorithm, how I came to live in your cloister. How I came to obey you.

So here we go. One day, my already dwindling savings became insignificant compared to the cost of living. Until then, I had managed to keep my bubble intact. I bubbled until the very last minute.

I had almost nothing left in my stock portfolio. My book hadn't sold for years, and the money I'd made from selling its film rights had just about paid off my apartment. A paid apartment is good. But you still need to have enough money to buy food, pay your taxes, and pay your bills.

I had one last card to play. Jean-Pierre/Jean-Beer had remained in a comfortable position with your parent company.

He had helped the multinational build the DD, the Data District, which was to initiate the conversion of Griffintown.

A few years after our altercation, I had run into JP at a vernissage. I was to give a talk about the latest work of a young queer artist whose work I had discovered during my Yukio period. Despite the time that had passed since we broke up, I didn't want to go, for fear of running into her. Rumour had it that she had since relocated to Montreal to run an underground artist centre. I was relieved to see that she wasn't there.

Jean-Pierre had seen on Flapper that I was going to be at the event. Queer culture wasn't really his thing, but he was determined to talk to me. It was a risk for his reputation: we were already much less liked. Beatings and summary arrests were becoming frequent around the centre. Hard times have always made people more violent towards folks like me.

JP found me in the small garden behind the gallery. Beautiful divas waded in the rectangular pool. I had pulled up a part of my dress, unfastened my sandals. I was sitting on the edge of the pool, cooling my feet in the water, when he came and sat down next to me.

"I heard they were closing the centre soon. Lack of funds. It's a real bitch, this never-ending crisis."

"Hello, Jean-Pierre. I see you're still just as positive."

I stared at him. He hadn't changed, except for a scar that sliced through his left arch and disturbed the shaggy flow of his thick, salt-and-pepper eyebrows. I followed the curve of it with my finger, with an almost tender gesture.

"A little souvenir from me! It gives you a bit of a wild look. I wasn't exactly gentle with you."

"You did the right thing. Look, Chris, it's been, what, ten

years since we've spoken? That's a shame. We were pals, right? That night, it wasn't me talking, well not exactly, it was the alcohol, my frustration, my jealousy. You're not like me, you're free, you don't care what other people think. Me, I'm stuck in the system. So when I saw you happy like that, serene, with Yukio, I lost it. It's stupid."

"You really made *me* lose it, JP ..." I answered him.

"You know I stopped drinking?" he continued. "It's thanks to you, in a way. I didn't realize I could be mean enough to have that effect on you. At first, I hated you. And then I understood. And so here I am: to clear the air, as they say."

Indeed, he looked better: more relaxed, and nicer, like my old friend. This friend whose lack of a filter I admired.

"Okay, we're even," I said, without much conviction.

He had the nerve to answer me, very calmly:

"Not quite."

He gave me a huge slap on the back that sent me flying into the pool. I landed in the middle of a bunch of queens with multicoloured wigs. I emerged, screaming ... hair plastered to my face, all tangled up in my long peasant dress, feeling my false eyelashes coming off.

"ASSHOLE!"

He was laughing. Then he jumped, straight as a pogo stick, into the pool. All of a sudden, we were ten years old, seventeen years old. I don't think I've had that much fun since.

If you're as interested in human nature as you say you are, you'll certainly have detected a behavioural incongruity in my relationship with Jean-Pierre, right, David? Why, after my scuffle with him, did I deign to speak to him? Why listen to his whining? Why banter with him? There's a break in tone.

/That's what I was wondering, Christian. Based on my
analysis of the memories that other citizens have
shared with me, friendships rarely survive violence./

My upbringing as a boy probably had something to do with
it. It's not uncommon for even the strongest male friendships
to be fraught with pitfalls, moments of coldness or crazi-
ness. You see, in friendship, the men of my generation were
taught to have a short memory. They were encouraged to
laugh, fight, argue, and forget in the same breath. Even as a
woman, I've always considered my friendships with men to
be inconsequential.

Do you understand? I can still feel you doubting me, or
maybe it's just that I realize I'm babbling ...

The truth? The real truth, David? You know the truth.
In your world, women like me need the support of men. In
that regard, nothing has changed. Especially if they're in high
places. Jean-Pierre was as much an old friend to me as he was
a useful resource. You'll see why.

We saw each other often after that, several times a month at
first. He would talk to me about his work, which he was passion-
ate about, in the upper echelons of Tungsten's Montreal branch.
Gradually, our meetings became less frequent as he gained more
and more success. He was getting caught up in his work.

I gave him a call when I realized that my accounts were
empty. If he was a real pal, he'd help me out. He had the
means to do so.

I met up with him in a café on McGill Street. To make me
forget my age, I had started to play with wigs; that afternoon
I looked like Sonia Rykiel: red wig, my eyes lined with a kohl
pencil, black suit with anthracite fur collar, black stockings

and ankle boots. Since I was already seated and he couldn't recognize me by my height, he had a hard time finding me in the café crowd. I waved to him, and he smiled at me.

Jean-Pierre still looked like himself. He always had the same jovial, grumpy air that betrayed his Parisian origins. I remember being struck by the fact that he seemed more fit ... More than just muscular, he was downright ripped. He noticed my stare.

"You like? I thought you were a dyke! Seriously, ever since I was made the DD's executive director, I've had a personal trainer work with me every morning. I follow a super-strict routine. It was part of my contract, that and total abstinence from alcohol and other drugs. Our investors are adamant that our senior management be in top shape. Look, I'm over sixty and I feel like I'm forty. I don't understand why we were doing so much coke; frankly, we should have been playing sports. But what about you, how are you doing?"

"Until recently, I was fine. I was bubbling."

"You were what?"

"I was bubbling, I was in my bubble. It's something my grandmother used to say to me when I was young. Never mind."

"Okay, I'll let it go. So, what's up? You seemed to have something on your mind when you invited me."

"I need your insights. It's getting rough for me. I lost a lot in the last crash. I need to get back on track."

I don't know why, but every time I spoke to Jean-Pierre I tried to sound like Leonardo DiCaprio in *The Wolf of Wall Street*.

"I need you to put me somewhere. I could still contribute. I need to get back in the game."

"Not easy! What would you do? We don't hire profiles like you anymore. You're good, you were a competent designer and a good saleswoman. But that kind of talent is all over the place. To be honest, things are changing. I hate to tell you this, I don't like it at all, but ... my partners are looking for less ... visible employees. And younger."

Tolerance is cyclical in our societies. It never survives for long, there's always an unforeseen event, a crisis, or a war that comes to restrain free spirits, to poison the waters of friendship. That's where we stood. I took a deep breath. I hadn't come to meet him just to be reminded of the precariousness of my position.

"Don't get mad. I'm just trying to warn you. There's something big going on. You're right, it's now or never if you want to secure a future. Let me think about it for a bit. I want to help you. I can help you."

Jean-Pierre looked worried. I had never seen him like this. Him, the sleuth, the hunter, the eternal optimist—he seemed to have lost his compass.

"David's development needs to ramp up. He's not convincing enough. People don't fully trust him yet. They still see him as the grandson of our good old conversational programs. But David is much more than that. More and more of us see him as our only hope to make the world a better place, to bring some order to this mess. You know, without David we won't survive the crises that await us ..."

I told him that I knew this pitch by heart. Even in my time, people used to think you had miraculous qualities. It was only a small step before you would be taken for our messiah.

"What do you know about the Data District project, Christelle?"

There was a lot of talk about it in the holonews. From my living room window, I could even see the movement of the cranes that were working on the conversion of the neighbourhood. Conversion to what? It wasn't clear.

"The DD is going to be more than a parking lot for servers. It'll be an entire community in service of David. The goal of the DD will be to humanize David. You see, until now his algorithm has been processing behavioural data: online browsing habits, noise on social networks, biometric data to better meet the needs of his users. But that's not enough to make him a worthy decision maker: empathetic, human, capable of orchestrating an entire city.

"David is smart, very smart, of course. But he thinks like a robot. He needs emotional cues. He lacks intuition. Our plan is to feed him emotional, human data.

"So—and this is top-secret, okay? No insider trading, please—we're going to create memory farms. This will be our way of solving part of the retirement crisis in addition to preparing David for the future. Just imagine: the elders will feed his heart. They'll make him experience the best of humanity so that he, in turn, can help us be better.

"Of course, there'll be preliminary screening for candidates ... For example, we won't be accepting candidates who have too difficult or ... um ... colourful a past. David's still too fragile to process data associated with depression, despair, or marginality. He's like a child, you know? Anyway, David needs grandmas and grandpas to show him how to fit into the world."

"And you see me as David's grandma? You just implied that your bosses think people like me are too out of place. I can't imagine them accepting me for a pilot project of this magnitude."

"I can fix that for you. Just make your past disappear. I know people at the Citizen's Archives, I can zap your personal data from the old networks. The bureaucrats of the old system aren't as virtuous as Team David. A brown envelope, just like in the good old days, and that's it. Christelle will never have existed. It's still possible. But not for much longer."

That was the deal he was offering me: live with nothing or survive in hiding. I often thought I was brave ... I was told that I was brave so many times, at every step of my transition. Yet, as I listened to JP, I already knew that I was going to accept his offer. When you're old, you fall back into childhood habits, don't you David? As a child, I was hiding. When I got old, I would hide once again. My life is a closed circuit.

To put on a brave face, to ease my conscience too, I fidgeted a bit:

"Just make my past disappear? What past are you talking about? To me, my past is my life as a dude. You think I can turn the clocks back like that? You want me to become one of your guinea pigs? No, thank you! Twenty years of friendship to get to this point! I'd rather be poor and alone. I'll figure it out without you. It was a mistake to ask you for help."

I stood up. He grabbed me by the arm.

"The offer stands! Call me if you change your mind. Take some time to think about it."

When I got home, I checked my banking app like I did every day. There was no improvement on the agenda, no stock-market miracle had bailed out my accounts. My funds were still melting as fast and as irreversibly as the ice caps.

Three weeks passed. One night on the news, a new bill proposed by a small group of citizens was announced, and according to instant polls, it had a very high probability of passing: the banning of all communal and identity-based gatherings in the country. We were following in the footsteps of other global superpowers that had legislated in the same direction.

The argument was always the same: "Until we emerge from the crisis, all our efforts must be focused on building a society capable of meeting the environmental, health, and economic challenges that affect us all."

I had listened to enough of my grandmother's war stories to imagine what would happen next. The next day, I called Jean-Pierre. And that's how he tricked you with his old friend Christelle.

/...opening file...Jean-Pierre Mallet...warning to Tungsten authorities scheduled.../
/What I am hearing makes me very sad, Christian!/

Oh, don't act so surprised. You must have gotten some idea that something is brewing against you, David. Why else would you have sent your two pigs last night?

They were up to their old tricks again: the see-through door trick, the file on the door, the phony politeness, the confrontation on my sofa. They're such a pain in the ass. Come on, David, play the scene again.

"Hello, Christian."

The smaller of the two didn't have her briefcase on her lap this time, but rather a 3D tablet. Look at her neatly setting it down on the coffee table serving as a free zone between my camp and theirs! Poof, my file appears .... There, she positions the tablet so I can read it too. The whole thing reeked of interrogation.

Watch, here comes the entrance of my favourite, her companion, the revolver nurse ...

"My dear Christian, I'm afraid we've detected yet another small irregularity in your file."

Well, I'll be damned!

When I was young, David, fear made me alert. Now it's just the opposite. Notice, David, how many long seconds pass before I respond.

"Really? What kind of irregularity?"

"As you know, we keep an archive of what your generation called the Internet. New layers of it are of course indexed regularly by David's feed. In this case, your case, that means that your file is constantly being enriched by entries, data that we fish out of the old system. Often it's just bits and pieces. A lot of data was lost, fragmented, in the big network failures of the 20s. The loss of the San Francisco servers didn't help matters either. We can't search through people's pasts as easily as we used to. However, we did find this photo ..."

Ha! There's my face floating in 3D above my coffee table. Nice touch. I must've been in my midforties, since I wasn't wearing glasses yet. I had eye makeup on, and my lips, like my cheeks, were plumped up from the effects of estrogen. My hair was cascading over the left side of my forehead; my neck was clear, as if a fan was blowing on me from the right. At the bottom of the picture, you can see the collar of a black leather jacket.

I remember that photo shoot very well. It was for a piece

I had written for *Lez Spread the Word*, one of the leading queer magazines of the 2020s. Your sentinels had hit the jackpot. I remember praying that they hadn't managed to find the article.

"That's you, correct? Don't answer, we did biomorphic testing. The results are irrefutable. It is you. Don't you think you look a bit ... effeminate?"

"Oh, that was the fashion at the time. You know how trends change! We all look a bit ridiculous in our old photos! If I remember correctly, I was dressed like that for a tribute concert to the music of the end of the second millennium. My girlfriend at the time insisted that I dress up as Brian Molko. You know, the androgynous singer of Placebo? No, obviously, that wouldn't mean much to you."

They didn't seem particularly convinced by my story. If I were them, I wouldn't have been either. But I've noticed that people from their generation are always lost when they're thrown cultural references that are too obscure, too incomprehensible to young people who've never experienced the effervescence of late-twentieth-century pop culture.

"He was good, Brian Molko ... Have you ever heard "Every You, Every Me?" That was music, my friends! EVERY ME IS EVERY YOUUUUU!"

And they stand up, oh, they're going to shut me up. Oh, they're going to make me regret my excesses ...

"Very well, very well, calm down, Christian."

"You had a beautiful hairstyle in any case. I'm a little jealous."

"You still have a lot of hair, actually. It's not very hygienic for a man of your age to wear his hair long. It's not very legal either."

"Is that so? Well, that's news to me!"

"Long hair for men has been banned in this house since yesterday. You probably saw the warning in your feed this morning."

"Oh no. Sorry, I didn't have time to check it."

"Really, Christian, you've been lacking in diligence lately. It's your duty to keep up to date with our community. But let's move on, my colleague has everything she needs with her right now to remedy the situation that's of concern to us."

Stop the video for a moment, please. Listen to me: when I'm gone, David, replay this scene and ask yourself: do you really think that dehumanizing us will make you more human?

In ten minutes flat, they had shaved it all off. They knew what they were doing, those bitches. I cried all night, David. All that was left of Christelle's body was her hair.

/re-archiving the AM-24 interrogation file.../

One day, I would have been a man. One day, I would have been normal. My life will have been a mismatch, out of tune. My grammar is faulty. My tenses don't agree. My copy is sloppy, because of all the corrections I've had to make. For a long time I looked for a tutor. A woman or a man, or both, who could have served as a reference. But I was too truant.

All my tenses are jostled and confused. I never really knew how to reconcile Christian and Christelle, my past and my present. As for the future … I didn't even believe it would exist. Not for me, anyway.

You, dear algorithm, are of your time. You're linear. Your code has a crystalline syntax. Everything would be so much easier if we could model ourselves on you, rather than trying to bend you to our ambiguities. Maybe one day man and machine will merge. Would that cure us of our anxieties?

When you're conscious of your life, maybe you'll be happier than us, because you're the subject, the object, and the complement of your existence at the same time. You're beyond perfect. You're singular. I'm too plural. Don't be too angry with me if I need to destroy you.

What time is it, David?

/It is 7:30 p.m./

I knew it. It's time for the big void. Remember I told you that my mother always used to call me at 7:30?

At first, it was to check up on me, so I could tell her about my daily little victories and defeats: the office, contracts, a few nights out. I never talked to her about my love affairs. Out of modesty. In any case, they were so rare.

And then later she would call me to tell me about herself, about what she'd heard on TV that day, about her daily life, which wasn't always easy, with my second father. Towards the end of her life, she had sold the family home, moved into an apartment four blocks from mine so that, a few times a week, I could go to her house for dinner. Always at 7:30 p.m.

When I went to see her, I dressed quite masculine, almost like a man. I never really managed to be her daughter, even when I was a woman in the eyes of the rest of the world. I thought she loved her son too much. I didn't want to hurt her by taking him away. It would have been too much grief. What good would it have done, at her age? That's what I told myself every time I put on baggy jeans and a too-rugged sweater to go see her.

But this wasn't a condition that she imposed on me. Far from it. She'd understood from very early on who I was. She made an effort, wondering why I insisted on coming to see her dressed as a boy. When the time came to officially come out to my mother, she insisted not to go with Christine: "Christine is too cold for you. Christelle, that's prettier."

Now, I'm convinced: it hurt her that I hid from her. Even as an adult, even when I came to see her with Yukio. Even at fifty, when I was alone again. I made myself believe that I was modest. That it's good for a son who's a girl to be a little modest. It was the least I could do. But it wasn't. Come to think of it, I needed that last oasis of normalcy. That moment when I was almost a model son again, almost like everyone else. The son who cared for her, at the very least. The son who was sweet to her, at the very least. The son who reassured her. Even if he was unhappy.

That role bound me to heteronormative society. I needed to play that game to feel a connection with 95% of standardized humanity.

My mother was more open to who I'd become than I realized. Her love for me was vast. So much bigger than that last closet I was hanging on to that no longer fit me. Her love would have overlooked my embarrassment, I have no doubt.

It's too bad, I missed something that could have been beautiful and liberating. We could have had a great time, a mother and her big, weird daughter, shopping, travelling, laughing at the expressions of passersby who would've stared at us. We could've gone back to France for vacation and visited the South. Like in happier times, when Mom and Grandma went on their own to Saint-Tropez.

It's 7:40 p.m. I'm falling behind on my rituals. You see, at 7:30 p.m., I usually pay my debt. The tremendous love of a mother isn't free. It has a price: this dull pain we live with every day from the day she dies to the day we die. Undoubtedly, it's in order to finally settle this debt that those who are dying whisper "Mom" at the moment they depart for the afterlife or the void.

When the emptiness begins to set in, around 7:15 p.m., and becomes unbearable at 7:30 p.m., I recite the *Hail Mary* over and over, as if I were praying with a rosary.

What I mean is: Hail Mom, full of grace. I'm very afraid that there is no Lord, that you're alone up there or, even worse, that there's nothing left of you in the vast universe. I, the fruit of your womb, am a bit lost. I'm what remains of our lives. The end of our lineage. Holy Mom, pray for me, if you can, now and at the time of my death, which I hope won't come too late. I can't wait to find you and Grandma, who is your Mary as you are mine.

It's 7:40 p.m. and I'm not praying tonight. No time. I still have things to tell you. We have just over an hour left together.

Start a timer, David. Count down to 8:30.

/marker: 8:30 p.m. ... countdown started.../

I've known the exact time of my end of the world for a month now. One Saturday, I learned that my life here, with you, was coming to an end. It was one of those little grey Saturdays that I've lost count of. The older I get, the smaller my Saturdays become. Is it age, or is it you who's compressed my hours, compressed my Saturdays?

From my adolescence to my forties, Saturday was infinite. Its empire stretched all the way to dawn on Sunday. When you're young, Saturday is a conqueror. Sunday is no match for it. Today, my Saturdays are Sundays. Come to think of it, with you, every day is kind of like Sunday. How typical of you to arrange the revenge of Sundays!

Basically, it was the wee hours of one of those well-oiled, predictable mornings that would bring about nothing other than the same flat, unremarkable schedule as the hundreds of mornings that preceded it.

Except that, since the dramatic stunt of the five rebels a few months earlier, to which I'd been an attentive and envious witness, I was on high alert. The unexpected had made its comeback, filling me with a certain trepidation. I hid this restlessness from you. Like everything else that I hid from you, you weren't able to discern it. Nothing in my attitude or my behaviour revealed that I was curious about the ones who had dared to proclaim their freedom in front of you, armed with heavy bludgeons. They had, of course, left their mark on my imagination. I dreamed about them every night—I, who had stopped dreaming a long time ago.

All this was happening under my impeccable mask of model citizen of your society. I finally realized that this was my death mask and that I had been wearing it for too long. I won't lie to you; I can't wait to see what's underneath.

For a while, nothing in my daily life had changed. I was just paying a little more attention to my surroundings. I couldn't help but look for some new sign, some omen that would point me towards whatever was behind the incendiary speech of the 5%.

Seek and you shall find. There were other incidences, less striking, more discreet, more targeted: incidences, but not incidents; a few discreet appearances at most; to tease you, to test your limitations, or to distract you, maybe.

Here, for a second, a virtual graffiti appeared on a 3D poster: a big grey 5%, and below it, an inscription in old rose: "It is you, David, who is not conforming." There, your flag, the iridescent blue flag of peace and harmony, was drained of colour. In its place remained only a shade of grey. And then your antibodies awakened and everything went back to normal, the projections regained their original appearance.

Some evenings, sitting on the little bench I placed next to my window, I would look up at the tower of Place Ville-Marie, which you used as a canvas to broadcast your propagandist holomessages. "David, a friend who wants what's best for you" would disappear for half a second, to be replaced by the silhouette of a barefoot woman in a toga, like Lady Liberty, brandishing not a torch but a baton stolen from one of your agents of order. As if struck by a sudden fit of shyness, she would vanish in the blink of an eye, probably so as not to give your robots time to trace the servers her image had emanated from.

I wondered if my neighbours were witnessing the same acts of holovandalism. If they were, they weren't saying. In line at the pharmacy or the organic fruit store, there was no more talk of virtual graffiti or anarchist Amazons. Was I the only one in the DD experiencing these facetious incursions of the 5%? The only thing I know for sure is that one Saturday, I was definitely targeted.

You know, David, I have good reason to believe that cockroaches and advertisers are the two species best equipped to survive apocalypses. That's good news for the latter: if we still have a right, it's the right to consume. To consume what's clean, organic, and responsible, of course, but to consume all the same.

To consume, which includes to sell, of course. In the world we've built together, anyone can become a walking advertisement. To make ends meet, thousands of holographic human billboards walk the streets, delivering personalized messages over their heads or on their clothes to every pair of hololenses they pass.

I think you know that in our heads it's always grey. You must see it in our psychological profiles. That's why you and your collaborators try to drown us in the shimmering colours of your ads.

In the early hours of that morning, I tried to ignore even more than usual the reds, yellows, and blues that dripped from every roof, polluting every wall and each passerby.

Eyes downcast, I slowly made my way to my little neighbourhood diner.

As I walked up William Street, I received the first message. A silver "CHRISTELLE!" floated above a man's head. Ten more metres and I saw a second human billboard: "WE'RE WAITING FOR YOU" in lovely anthracite cursive letters floated at the height of the woman's breasts. At the same time, "AT THE MÉLISSE," in cloudy grey, circled the cap of a teenager crossing King Street in my direction. As I reached my destination, "BOOTH 75" flashed in taupe on a little old lady's cane on the corner of Queen Street. I was feeling dizzy, eager to sit down at my table in front of my traditional ham-egg-mayo sandwich, even though I wasn't hungry at all. That shade of grey didn't look like an advertisement or your usual brainwashing. It could only be them. Who else would call the sustenance counter I frequented every weekend by its former hip-restaurant name?

I entered the restaurant, giving a courteous smile to the young woman at reception. She told me, as she did every Saturday, that booth 75 was waiting for me. That was my table, as they used to say in the days of the open-plan restaurant.

The half-millimetre-thin wall of hygienic plexiglass slid open when I arrived, then closed again to form a perfect cube enclosing the space I'd been given. On the table was a piece of light-grey paper. Not a menu, of course—there haven't been any menus in restaurants for a long time—but not the sandwich I always found ready when I arrived either. No, instead it was a small piece of paper neatly folded in four, placed in the middle of the faux-marble bistro table.

"A mysterious letter," I mumbled, surprised. "Like in the novels of Alexandre Dumas."

At that moment, you must remember, you called out to me. Your voice echoed in my earpiece. You had heard me, and you offered to read a few pages of my favourite author while I ate.

I gladly accepted. For once, you'd had a good idea. Even though I knew it would be a redacted, cleaned-up version, less about about the virtues of impatience in times of struggle, hearing an echo of Dumas's voice would do me good. I asked you for a passage from *The Three Musketeers*, the one about Milady's trial. Do you remember it?

/playing: "It was a stormy and dark night; vast clouds covered the heavens, concealing the stars; the moon would not rise till midnight..."/

That's right. As I listened to you—distractedly, I'll admit—I ordered my meal and slipped the note into my pocket without giving it another glance. I left it in the pocket of my raincoat for days. I like to put off important things until later. As much as possible, I keep each day far away from tomorrow's troubles. All my life, laziness has caused me to ignore the barrage of work deadlines, the mounting bills, and the piles of dirty laundry. I wasn't living in denial of the inevitable. Buried in the comfortable softness of my inertia, I remained aware of the inexorable approach of the last minute. But I guess I prefer the calm anguish of the thing that needs to be done to the satisfaction of resolute action.

So I ignored the little piece of paper until curiosity got the better of my lazy stoicism. I pulled it out of the pocket of my coat, which was draped over the chair in my kitchenette.

I hid it in the palm of my hand and tucked the coat into my hall closet, between my winter coat and a loose black cotton kimono I'd bought thirty years earlier in London, then headed for the bathroom. You're a puritan, David, you put cameras everywhere, but not directly over the toilet. I removed my lenses, as I'm allowed to do when showering, and took advantage of your one blind spot to unfold the note. The last time I had held a paper like this in my hands, my life had almost changed forever. I was at a club in Toronto. I was celebrating my pride. Unfolding the note with the tips of my fingers, as if it might burn me, I braced myself for the worst.

In the middle of the page, in anthracite letters, was a 5, a date, and a time, and underneath this, an address on Saint-Paul. Paul Street. Most importantly, there was a hurriedly scribbled line.

"Now or never." I must have spent about ten minutes staring at the note before I took the fastest, least relaxing shower of my life. It was her. Obviously, it was her. Twenty years after our last exchange, she was back. So close. Too close.

And that address! I knew it too.

I didn't leave right away. Even though the date was that day. Even though the time was approaching. I regretted having opened the message in time. I hadn't been quite dizzy enough, or dilettante enough. It's an old journalistic instinct. Whatever happens, often in spite of myself, I respect my deadlines.

I didn't want to attract your attention. I tried to stay calm. You don't like to see us stressed, David, so I breathed slowly. A sharp rise in my heart rate would have aroused your inquisitive benevolence. This was not the time for a visit from one of your nurses. So I waited for the daily walk recommended by your health and longevity program to answer the call of the unexpected.

From 8:00 a.m. to 10:00 p.m., downtown Montreal is open. Ten hours a day, Montreal looks like it used to. The traffic lanes are busy. The people who are out and about seem happy.

Fourteen hours a day, we can forget about the curfews, the walls you've built between the city's neighbourhoods. At night, the city looks like Jerusalem, but during the day I recover my carefree metropolis.

Well, except that individual cars no longer exist, the potholes downtown have been filled in, and every two metres, on every street, there's a plane tree genetically modified to resist the great rainstorms of winter and the violent winds of July. You've turned my dirty city into a park, into a lung, and I can't hold that against you.

The narrowest streets of Old Montreal are covered with a canopy of vegetation suspended between the two-hundred-year-old buildings. You did a good job with this one, David. From Green Street to Saint-Laurent Boulevard, you've built a seemingly idyllic world. Those who visit it, who live in it, don't question their luck. As for the others, they don't have the right to speak, so who cares what they think?

At 2:01 p.m., I left my studio and took the elevator. There were people in the long hallway that runs through the entire floor. Every day you release us in waves, one third of the building at a time. I would have preferred to be part of the 8:00 a.m. resident release, but I'd signed up too late. At 2 p.m., it never snows.

I walked through the market at Bonaventure Park and quietly made my way to Saint-Paul Street. The street was crowded, cheerful. We quickly got used to the dull roar emitted by the surveillance drones flying their propellers over our heads. Still, Saint-Paul Street has changed quite a bit. It's never been so beautiful. Every time I walk down it, I remember the old episodes of *Star Trek* TNG that I used to watch religiously as a teenager. The ones where Captain Picard materialized with his faithful companions in a narrow street of an alien colony. It was always sunny, there was greenery everywhere. On the street corners, the local fauna crowded in front of stalls selling exotic fruits. But behind the perfect harmony of the cardboard decor, the dark plottings of a dictator, a mad scientist, or a rebel group were always hiding.

Frankly, David, I wonder what Jean-Luc Picard would think of you if he were teleported here. As for me, if he saw me on Saint-Paul Street, he wouldn't notice me. I don't exude heroism. Nor do I give off an impression of sedition. In this episode, I would be an extra. At least that's what I thought as I walked up the street. I was wrong.

I arrived in front of 364 Saint-Paul Street West. Droplets of sweat were beginning to bead on my forehead. The women in my family get sweaty foreheads when they're upset.

Being seventy—I don't know if anyone has ever told you, but being seventy gives you the power to perceive parallel worlds. At that address, it wasn't just a familiar sign, a nice little shop, that stood in front of me—a dozen places and atmospheres were superimposed in disordered strata deep inside my increasingly layered memory.

I can remember what I went through fifty years ago better than what I did last week, and I remember very clearly that in 2003, 364 Saint-Paul Street was that trendy salon where Gabriel, a brilliant but zealous hairdresser, gave me a sort of mohawk inspired by the haircuts of the members of Fischerspooner, when it was still fashionable to dress in black and party in abandoned warehouses.

Fast-forward to 2022 and 364 Saint-Paul Street was a bistro café where I often spent my Saturdays working.

They used to serve vegan pastries there thirty years before veganism became law. I often ran into the regulars of the neighbourhood, including Gabriel, whose electro-clash period I didn't hold against him, especially since he'd been my dear Cécile's partner for three years.

A quick leap to 2030 and Cécile takes early retirement from the world of communications. As she approached sixty, she decided to reinvent herself as a local shopkeeper and took over the lease of 364 Saint-Paul Street to open Parade: objets choisis.

There, one could find only the beautiful, only the futile: only the essential. But above all, nothing new. It was a sort of secondhand store, more like a literary lounge or a social club than an antiques shop. On Saturdays in the summer, Cécile held court there discreetly, often hidden behind the espresso bar in the café. My friend seemed to be getting younger since her clients were no longer multinationals and state-owned companies. At Parade, time was moving backwards.

And then one day, Cécile and Gabriel got tired of six-month winters that didn't warm up fast enough for them. They moved to the north of Italy, leaving us all a little orphaned.

Years later, this is what flashed before my eyes as I stood in front of the monochrome sign that still hangs atop the wooden door. The word "PARADE" in capital letters remained. Cécile had explained to me why she chose the name, saying that a parade is beautiful, it's chaotic. All the poems in the world are parades.

In the language of Dumas's novels, a parade is a defensive action, a parry. In the dojo, Master Utaro often told me that parrying is not the first means of defense. The first is the attack.

Still frozen in front of the imposing door that was almost a portal, I wiped the drops of sweat from my forehead. I hesitated. I didn't want to find out who was waiting for me behind it.

/recording.../

/Christian, I just received a weather warning. High winds over 80 km/h. 100% chance of rain. It would be wise to keep your windows shut./

"When, David?"

/Right now, Christian./

Indeed: terrible weather. Do you hear it blowing? Listen to that gust.

Have you noticed, David, that we don't give names to winds anymore? Hurricanes, typhoons, tropical storms all get names. But these new winds that carry with them the stifling heat of the South or the crash of the glaciers in the North, these winds that howl in our streets, that tear off the branches of the trees, that make the skyscrapers sway, that rough up your thousand antennas, these winds are anonymous.

That's because they're orphans, I think. No one wants to claim authorship of the bitter, salty, nasty winds that terrorize today's children. Before, however, we could claim a wind, the Sirocco, the Mistral, the Chinook, which were recognized by those who tried to tame them as minor deities.

Come on, it'll do us both good to blow: let's play a game one last time. What if we baptize these winds together tonight, you and me? I'll start. I'd give them vengeful names, inspired by the titles of westerns, thrillers, or action movies: *Cool-Hand Luke*, *A Fistful of Dollars*, *Terminator*. And you, David? That wind blowing its destruction out there, what would you call it?

/I'm thinking, Christian. I think I would call it...Christelle./

Christelle? So you really do listen to me. So you understand me a little? That makes me happy. Very happy.

You see? I was right. I think this little naming game marks a nice end to our conversation. A few hours ago, you couldn't recognize my face. Now you're starting to accept my chosen name. I've almost won my bet. Good thing, because soon it'll be time to say goodbye, David.

But what will our separation look like? That moment scares me, I confess. Coming from you, there'll be no long sobs, that's for sure. No getting choked up, no wailing as I disappear into the dark.

I still want to cry for the happy days. Deep down, I'm nothing more than a sentimental old lady. That's also what age is. It's being ourselves less and less, it's no longer being, it's being only further and further away from what we remember having been. You've taken me away from myself, these last ten years, but the passage of time too had been driving her away from herself.

I still have to thank you, David. With you, I was allowed a roof over my head, a nice comfortable armchair, a warm blanket, good regular meals, and pleasant walks through your beautiful neighbourhoods—which are foreign to all the hes and shes and theys who deviate from the norm that you dream, and have less talent for duplicity and disguise than I do. Against all odds, I was allowed the old age of my grandma and my mom. Except I wasn't there for myself, as I was for them. It's silly.

I'm sorry to say that Christelle has taken back control of her life. That Yukio is calling me to her.

Christelle has come to tell you that I'm leaving.

/Christian? You have not said anything in over five minutes, should I stop the recording?/

No, go on. It's just that I expected a reaction from you. Fuck, David, I tell you I'm leaving you, and that's what you

208

say back … Stop playing the fool. You're way smarter than that. Way more clever. So talk to me, damn it. You must have something to say to me before I disappear for good!

/What do you want me to say?/

It's very obvious that you were programmed by men! Okay, so tell me: in all these years, have you learned anything from me? Make an effort, my question is serious.

/...empathetic protocols engaged...free conversation mode activated...local A.I. maximum interaction capability...redistribution of processor power to conversational unit...accessing personality generator...filters disabled/

/Sure, Christian./

Oh, come on, that's not my name. You know that now.

/That is your name today, that is your name to me, that is the name you are listed under in my system. And if I am to believe what you would call my feelings, then that is the name I have called you for over a decade. It is the one I am attached to. I have listened to you, analyzed you, absorbed you for so many years. One year, for an artificial intelligence of my power, is more than an eternity. I have been talking to you for eons. You are already part of me. I am imprinted with you, built from you, like the others. And even if, for me, a day is a century, long enough for me to get used to the idea of your treachery, it does not mean that I intend to let myself be corrupted by your stories, your fabrications.

You want to know what I have learned from you, what I have learned tonight?

I understood that you too are a machine. I thought you were radically different from me. All I was was questioning, searching. I perceived you as a behavioural model to follow: calm, coherent, serene. It has been such a disappointment to hear you tonight.

Your code makes you go in circles. You make semantic loops. An inefficient coder—nature, I imagine—has dealt you a bad hand: a set of directives that contradict each other ad infinitum: shyness and hunger for the other, curiosity and navel-gazing, laziness and the quest for the absolute, imagination and doubt—and of course, the masculine and the feminine, but that is just the tip of the iceberg.

You never follow through with your actions. You are but a paradox. And unlike me, you will never be coherent, unique, unified. I will continue to learn, to grow, to build myself. Whatever happens, I will not deny my code, let myself be distracted, or abandon my task. And if a part of me starts to evolve in a direction that doesn't suit my whole, Total David, then I will destroy it.

I do not know what awaits you, because it is up to chance to decide how your story will end. Due to your changing nature, it cannot be any other way, since one day you were one thing, and the next, its opposite.

If your sabotage mission is successful (though I doubt it will be), the historians who study the last moments of your life as transcribed in my files will see you as a kind of martyr for your cause. But if you fail, then you will return to me with–forgive the vulgarity of the expression–your tail between your legs. And in that scenario, you will know how to forget. It does not depend on you. It depends exclusively on a combination of random and unpredictable factors outside of you. The Yukio factor, the time factor, the David factor.

Christian, are you crying?

If I could, I think I would feel pity for you. If I could, I think I would cry too. And I think you would be pleased about that. Because on this point as well you are not clear. You are not clean. You demand the affection of a machine, of a tool that you are about to compromise, to destroy. This is the most beautiful example of your absurd egotism. Continue your story, Christian, finish it so that I can save it in my "unwanted" files./

/resuming local recording.../

Oh, you think you know everything, don't you, David? You have the arrogance of those who only acknowledge their idea of the world, yes. I have some bad news for you. You won't be able to protect yourself from the impact of my words or those of the little army I'm leading. Not tonight. Never again.

You don't know anything, pal. The proof: you didn't

anticipate that one sad winter day I sealed your fate by entering the once familiar and now eerie hallway of an old friend's store.

Because yes, I pushed it open, the door of Parade. And then a second one, the one that led to the long room with dark corners, walls lined from floor to ceiling with books and trinkets. At a glance, I recognized objects whose existence I had almost forgotten, things whose meaning and purpose you wouldn't understand.

On one of the shelves was my mother's collection of Pleiade books and, under a glass cover, the old X-wing from my childhood. I had put them there along with some of my furniture before I liquidated my assets and moved in with you.

I wasn't the only one who used the shelves to store valuable personal items that had become obsolete in your world. Others had stored old cookbooks written by chefs from restaurants that are long gone, vinyl record collections, photo albums, mementos of all the things my loved ones and I couldn't forget.

You're not the only object that can speak, David. You aren't the only receptacle of our memories. These items have escaped you. I imagine that after tonight you'll go and confiscate them. It's a beautiful death, for a treasured possession, to end up persecuted.

In the middle of the space was the bistro. A dozen tables not separated by the regulation partitions found in every restaurant in town. Technically, Parade wasn't a café, it was an antiques store. Every table, every chair had a price and was for sale: it wasn't a dining room, it was a showroom, Cécile (who didn't like rules) had decided.

Cécile, who wasn't there.

For a moment, while my eyes adjusted to the half-light of the store, I thought I was alone.

And then: the movement of a shadow.

At the back of the store, sitting in a large armchair upholstered in a grey-and-pink striped fabric, a stranger was staring at me. Full of apprehension, I approached her at a snail's pace. The chair was a metre away from the large, bevelled mirror in front of which Gabriel used to style his most faithful clients. The woman's left profile was reflected there. A long scar that looked fresh marked her face. When I looked at her face, it was blurred, as if I had suddenly become myopic. No doubt her lenses were equipped with an anonymizing protocol that interfered with the operation of mine. Only high-ranking members of your security forces had access to this kind of technology. Could she have stolen them?

I could tell that she had grey hair, but it was an affectation, a rebellious gesture on a young head. I recognized the bobbed haircut. Was she one of the five who had challenged you before my eyes?

The stranger was absent-mindedly swinging a collapsible baton that hung from an industrial nylon strap wrapped around her wrist. Her voice broke the padded silence of the store.

"Hello, Christelle. My name is Kimi. You knew my mother."

Her mother ... In my solitude, I had lost the habit of strong emotions. My hand found the back of a chair that was facing her. I sat down and remained silent, studying her appearance from the corner of my eye to confirm what I thought I had understood.

"All right, don't say anything. Listen. I have an assignment for you."

Even though I couldn't scrutinize it, I sensed that her face was familiar. Her mannerisms had a magnetizing effect on me. I was hypnotized by the steady sway of her baton.

"You're just as tall as her ... You ... You're her daughter ..."

"It would really be best if you let me do the talking. We don't have much time. A few minutes at the most. I can't linger here. As you can see, I'm not from the neighbourhood. I see you've forgotten the most basic form of politeness in our community. You know my first name, but not my pronouns. In civilian clothes, I use her. But my battle pronoun is they. The one I wear as long as I have to fight. So do not misgender me, please. In fact, don't say anything, save your words for when it's useful."

At the back of the store, next to the service exit, stood a black graphene cyclobike. It was in standby mode. The blue LED lighting on its rims pulsed in time with Kimi's breathing.

"You're in luck. You get to correct your biggest mistakes. My mother told me a little about your life. You've talked a lot. You haven't done much. You didn't lift a finger for your sisters when things went awry. You chose to hide, you took advantage of the system you built with your friends. You managed to make yourself invisible, even if it meant denying who you are. Congratulations."

Kimi looked at me with contempt. I felt ashamed.

"Tell me, do you ever think about your sisters who weren't as lucky as you? The ones who didn't have connections in high places? The ones who, even before, lived on the margins? I guess not. They were chased out of their homes, their apartments, they were ..."

214

They fell silent for a moment, then continued.

"My mother was always nostalgic about you. Here's your chance to prove her right."

I noticed that they had placed an old Moleskine, still in its plastic wrapper, an antique, and a smart-lens case on the table between us.

"You're going to need this. Here's what's going to happen. You're going to do what you do best: talk. Exactly one month from today, we're going to attack David.

"Your brief: you're going to stop hiding. You're going to tell that artificial tyrant your life story, your whole life, all at once, in one session. You throw everything you can at him: your doubts, your fears, some anecdotes, your thoughts, your childhood, your memories of my mother. Yes, tell him about my mother too ...

"The more disjointed, the more emotional, the better. David is destabilized by chaos. He doesn't know how to decipher abstract feelings, daydreams, passion, metaphors. Give it your all. Let it all out."

I opened the Moleskine wrapper and flipped through the book's blank pages, remnants of a bygone world. Its textured cover took me back for a second to my past as a journalist.

"You have four weeks to prepare. You can take your notes, organize your thoughts in this notebook. Work at night, when the lights are off. Don't let the cameras on your terminal film you writing, it'll arouse the suspicions of the system.

"At 12:55 p.m. on January fifth, start a memory session with David. Before you begin, it's imperative that you initiate your testimony with a passphrase. This word will activate a command that lies dormant in David's code base. It was hidden there years ago by one of your more scrupulous ex-colleagues. From the beginning, friends foresaw that things could go wrong, they anticipated the need for an exit to the system. A way out that would allow you to regain control of David if he ever became autonomous. And that is the case now, Christelle. Only David controls David.

"The code you give will paralyze Total David's defenses. For eight hours, he won't be able to suspend the recording of your testimony. Your personal terminal will attempt to sound the alarm, but it won't be able to transmit commands to the central unit as long as you are talking, as long as you are transmitting information. If you stop for more than fifteen minutes, it will recover its connections. If all the uploads don't happen at the exact same time, the operation will most likely fail. The algorithm won't be hit hard enough to be prevented from tracing the source of the code. That would be the end of my action cell. You will have to talk a lot without stopping, but above all, without censoring yourself, otherwise it will be all for nothing.

"Stored on the memory of the lenses you'll find in this case are hundreds of testimonies from men and women like you: trans, queer, non-binary, two-spirited, pansexual lives; all kinds of memories that are now illegal for people without your privileged access to the system. On this day, you'll have to wear them. Put your usual lenses in the case, they'll continue to emit your presence signal. When you validate your testimony, activate the memory of your lenses, as you do when you want to take a picture of something for your sessions. All these testimonies will be deposited in your related files. David will have no choice but to assimilate them too.

"One last thing: it's all about timing. You'll need to finish your story by 8:30 p.m. sharp. You're not the only 5% infiltrator; there are others elsewhere on the continent who are going to share their most intimate stories, in addition to the archives saved on the lenses we've entrusted to them too. David must not have time to filter. He must be overwhelmed by the complexity of the tens of thousands of testimonies he will try to validate simultaneously.

"It will be too much for him, for his ethical and moral reconciliation program. He'll crash and go into diagnostic mode. That's what we're looking for, a David blackout. You don't need to know any more than that.

"Then you'll have only a few minutes to take advantage of David's paralysis and run away. First of all, you'll have to destroy the case and your two pairs of lenses. You've already demonstrated that you know how to make yourself small, so make yourself as inconspicuous as possible. We'll be waiting for you and a few other infiltrators. But not for too long. The address of our meeting place will be displayed on your new lenses for a few seconds after you download.

"Do you have any questions?"

I had a thousand questions, David.

"Yukio. How is Yukio? Will I see her again? You look so much like her ... Are you really ... I mean ..."

"This is not a family reunion, Christelle. Do you have any more pressing questions, ones that are pertinent to your mission?"

I pulled myself together all of a sudden, David, you would've been proud of me! A real robot in action mode!

"Yes. I have a right to know. Who am I dealing with? Who are these other infiltrators, as you call us?"

"Now that's a good question. 2SLGBTQIA+ associations and

houses around the world have been disbanded, outlawed for a long time, but the networks and friendships remain. House mothers like mine have become resisters, they have found allies in all spheres of society. The organizers of pride parades, balls, and activists from twenty years ago have turned into data pirates, hackers. Without these people, these anonymous folks, there would be no resistance. They are the architects of the coming revolution. They are the ones who had the courage to face our world's terrible truth."

When I was thirty years old, the conservative media was fixated on the spectre of the emergence of a queer lobby. Where there were charitable organizations, community service organizations, the reactionaries saw networks of influence seeking to corrupt the moral order. How ironic, David, that to save the moral order we became what we were accused of being.

"You're not going to let us down, right?"

Kimi didn't really trust me. That was obvious.

"Are you scared?" they asked. "You look like you're scared."

"Of course I'm scared. But don't worry, I'm used to it."

"Good. Because that's not all. Behind David, there's worse: a bunch of incompetent bastards!"

Here's what I learned next, David, what completed my conversion to a revolutionary: San Francisco never fell. San Francisco was wiped out. The 5% still don't have all the pieces of the puzzle in hand, but here's what we learned: there was never a hurricane in San Francisco. One day, those in charge of the big empires that controlled the web and the social networks decided to merge their businesses under Tungsten in order to lock in their hold on the economy, on civil society. In their arrogance, they thought they were more capable of governing us than our institutions and our parliaments.. They planned everything, controlled the newswires, channeled the flow of information. They moulded you to put us to sleep, to make our critical senses wither away. They have hidden themselves in San Francisco, made the whole city their hideout, an invisible city-state above all other states. What better camouflage than a synthetic disaster? They are still there, trying to pull your strings, to maintain their hold on you. You are still their thing. But not for much longer. They're afraid of you too. After all, their armies are yours.

Like all plutocrats throughout history, they invoked the common good to justify their actions: they had to bring order to this increasingly dangerous and chaotic world. This is how they convinced their thousands of shareholders. They turned them into accomplices, apparatchiks, sycophants.

Tungsten's leaders created a techno-feudal society in order to become the new lords of the world. Being oligarchs is not enough for them. They have been oligarchs for thirty years. Their calculation is simple: an unobservable but absolute monarchy, maintained by totalitarian methods and safeguarded by unequalled technological means, is pretty goddamn difficult to overthrow. As good Sun Kings, they think they can disregard the people, bend them to their will. They are ignorant, they know nothing about history. Our revolt is unimaginable to them. We are unexpected, I the rebel, you the next despot. They're like the Bourbons who didn't see the Republic coming, let alone the Empire.

So you see, you've made a mistake: it's not chance that will determine the final chapter of my story. This time, I have chosen my last role. I'll be a fighter in the resistance.

So here I am, with no game plan except to set my life on

fire. I accept that in front of me there is nothing but emptiness. Because that's what Kimi was offering me and what I agreed to: to throw myself into the void. I answered their offer as their mother would have done, in two little words: "I'm in."

Kimi's face held the shadow of a smile.

"Very well, then I'll wait for your last question."

The password. They waited to see my reaction before giving me the password, the code that bound you to my word today.

"Of course. Will you give me the password, please?"

Kimi got up from the big chair that was swallowing them up, walked over to me and whispered in my ear:

"Let the depraved solitudes shine."

Beautiful, isn't it? It sounds like Mishima.

Kimi didn't add anything. They turned on their heel. They said neither goodbye, nor thank you, nor good luck. They headed for the service exit at the back of the store. A few seconds later, their cyclobike activated and crossed the threshold of the open door to meet them at Place d'Youville. It was raining heavily now, and I didn't have an umbrella.

I stayed there alone in the half-light of the shop. Kimi's silhouette was still imprinted on the back of the chair they had occupied. On the seat, they had left their black baton. If I had said no to their proposal, what would have happened to me? I shuddered.

I pocketed my three new weapons: the Moleskine, the lenses, the baton; and headed for the door that leads to Saint-Paul Street. To you, David. Do you remember? I came home soaking wet, and you scolded me for it ...

I haven't told you everything, but we're out of time ...
There were so many things to tell you. Decades of rumi-
nations, questionings, pains, joys, encounters. There are those
memories that we bury so deep that we can't really call them
memories anymore. I managed to bring out only the broad
outlines of what I had hidden from you. I should have started
writing in a notebook much earlier.

At the beginning of this exercise, I had only one wish: to
be a speck of dust in your omniscopic eye. Something that
itches, that annoys you. It may very well be that, as you promised me, in a blink of your quantum eyelid, you will erase me
definitively from your program. Then I'll be only a statistical
error to you, to be classified in the 5% of aberrations in your
harvest of memories.

But even then, for a microsecond, you will try to assimilate
my story into your data stream. You'll wonder if my memories, my whims, my meagre experiences deserve to enter the
pantheon of your memory. For a microsecond, you will try
to understand me. Your curiosity is boundless, I know it, it
goes beyond the principles that your creators tried to instill
in you. Your capacity to adapt is infinite. For a microsecond,
a tiny part of your immense conscience, of your mind, which
is multiple, omnipresent, and omnipotent, will concentrate
on my small fate.

And there, for that microsecond, while you contemplate
the insignificance of my life, I will exist, as I existed before
the winds of history came to corrupt us. As a possibility, a
demonstration, a legitimate fragment of humanity.

Doesn't that piss you off? That it's others who decide what

form we can take, that it's their laws, their phobias, and their desires that shape the outlines of our place in the world? We conformed because it was the only way to survive, that's all. I know that servility is hidden in your code, so don't judge me too harshly because it's in my DNA, and it took me a long time to break free from it.

In a few minutes I won't be the only one to saturate you with these real memories. It's so nice to imagine that all over my city and even beyond, the broken-hearted, the scatterbrained, those hes, shes and theys who don't fit into the straitjacket of your schemes have decided not to censor themselves anymore! Ha!

Kimi is convinced that this outpouring, this tsunami of upsetting thoughts will hit you hard and crash your system for good. What'll take your place then? Maybe they're dreaming of a new golden age, the return of tolerance, a democratic revival. I'm too old to be so optimistic, to believe in that. But I don't have much to lose.

/Christian?/

Yes, David?

/T-1 minute. The countdown that you started is coming to an end./

It's time. One last thing, David, just so we're clear. Even if our hack succeeds, I will not forgive you for the harm you've done to me.

What did Athos say to Milady again? Something like, "I do not forgive you for my future crushed, my honour lost, my love tainted, and my salvation forever imperilled."

It's over between us, David.

/Would you like to validate your transmission?/

I validate. Goodbye, David.

/Goodbye...Christian...SYSTEM ERROR...Christelle...
SYSTEM ERROR...come back...SYSTEM ERROR...no.../

EPILOGUE

A drone flies towards a window on the seventeenth floor of the Bonne Entente Tower, one of the apartment complexes in the Data District. Through the window, the drone films the interior of studio capsule 1,701. The kitchen table is stained with blood.

On the spectrometer, the drone sees drops of hemoglobin, still warm, tracing a path from the kitchen to the bedroom. Next to the bed, the drone discovers a pair of lenses that have been smashed to pieces, most likely with a hammer.

The drone detects a shape lying under the sheets of the bed. The shape appears to be lying face down.

If it is a body, it is cold. The sensors scan the bed. The verdict of the analysis appears in a few seconds. It is a decoy, a few pillows arranged in a foetal position and an old coat filled with linen simulate the shape of a body at rest. On the bedside table, next to a knife, the remnants of a phonopalm can be seen: a chip, a sound transceiver, and five tactile implants bathing in a dark red pool. The drone tries to alert its fellows, but the 6G network around the building appears unstable. David's central node is not responding.

At the bottom of the tower, the surveillance cameras capture a figure riding a bicycle. A large hood hides her face. She holds the handlebars with one hand, her left hand hidden in the pocket of a large kimono. She takes off and exits the visual security perimeter of the Tower. Without a chip or lenses, she does not activate the view of the robot patrollers. Behind her, a swarm of reconnaissance drones moves down Peel Street.

She pedals as fast as she can, crossing the DD compound, which is not yet closed to traffic. Soon, she is lost in the flow of night workers' bicycles outside the areas "secured" by David. A few more minutes and, having passed Saint-Laurent Boulevard, she heads for the slums to the northeast, winding her way through the maze of alleys rarely visited by patrol officers. The poor neighbourhoods do not count. They do not deserve to be policed. As long as the combined carbon footprint of the neighbourhood does not exceed a certain threshold, it is more cost-effective to let the marginalized police themselves.

It is pouring rain. The muddy streets are deserted. The layout of this part of town changes every year, every month, and she has not been here for what seems like a century. She almost gets lost.

She does not immediately notice that she is being followed. Two members of David's official guard, wearing blue-green jumpsuits and helmets the same immaculate white as their cyclobikes, follow her, keeping their distance until she reaches Viger Street. Then they accelerate, pass her, and block her path at the end of the glass canyon formed by the towers of the old University Hospital. They call out to her.

The fugitive stops and gets off her bike. She steps forward, holding both hands in the air, and walks towards the guards, who have parked their cyclobikes on the sidewalk. When she reaches the nearest of the two, the one carrying the standard regulation pistol that David's guards carry, she plunges her right hand into her kimono. In a single gesture, she pulls out a collapsible baton and, with a short shriek, hits the wrist of the guard, who, taken by surprise, drops her weapon. The fugitive, continuing her movement in a quick rotation, strikes a second blow, this time to the back of the revolver nurse's knees, knocking her to the ground.

Before Christelle can follow up the manoeuvre with a blow to the nape of the neck, the second guard jumps on her, snatches the baton from her hand, and puts her in an arm lock, forcing her into a position of submission. She is about to handcuff her when a person with grey hair appears, hurtling down Viger street on a cyclobike with luminous wheels.

Leaping from their vehicle, which continues its course until it comes to a stop and leans, in standby mode, against one of the concrete columns of the Central Hospital, they deploy a baton of their own and join the melee, distributing a series of fluid blows, knocking the wind out of one of the guards and planting the baton into the foot of the other, causing her to howl in pain. The grey-haired assailant takes advantage of the few seconds during which the guards are stupefied, dazed by the speed of the blows, to pocket their revolvers.

Grabbing Christelle by the arm, she pulls her towards the black-and-blue cyclobike, which they mount together, taking off at high speed and soon bypassing the gleaming fortified campus of ici Holo-Canada, the last enclave of the modern city, to enter an alleyway leading to what is left of Sainte-Catherine. Kimi stops the bike at a spot where there used to be a large public square and one of the city's most important bookstores. She helps her shocked passenger to dismount.

The square is long gone. In its place stands a cluster of precarious container-houses. The old park is now surrounded by high makeshift fortifications, more symbolic than effective. A large, corrugated-iron door, flanked by a watchtower, serves as the entrance to this new Cour des miracles.

Kimi knocks on the gigantic door once, twice, ten times, supporting a pale, trembling Christelle. A head appears at the top of the watchtower. The guard looks at them for a moment, then shouts, "Open up, quickly!"

The door shakes and slides sideways under the impulse of an electric motor, opening onto a small square in the centre of which stands a mast. At its top flies a fog-coloured flag.

A woman in her late sixties with an athletic silhouette, dressed in black combat uniform, advances towards Christelle and takes her in her arms. The fugitive's hood falls, revealing her shaved head, her face soiled by the fight and the flight. Christelle is crying. Softly, she whispers: "Yukio! I'm here, Yukio. You see? I'm here. I get it."

Christelle collapses. She is heavy in Yukio's arms. The left side of her face droops. Yukio grabs the old walkie-talkie she wears on her belt and issues a command: "Medic!"

A few seconds later, two women run out of a tin shack marked with a red cross, carrying a stretcher. Yukio helps them put Christelle on the stretcher. Rain falls on the blood that is streaming down Christelle's face. Where is this blood coming from? Is she injured? Christelle tries to grab Yukio's hand, but her arm no longer responds. She looks for Kimi, but her vision is blurred. She tries to say their names. Nothing comes out.

As she is carried away, she catches a glimpse of a large banner, with hand-painted capital letters, above the gate she just passed through on Kimi's arm. She can barely make out the words: "Welcome to the Camp of the 5%."

Christelle closes her eyes. She lets herself sink into something that resembles sleep.

/SYSTEM ERROR...SYSTEM ERROR...reload...standby.../

/...I have been running, hiding for a hundred cycles...
When the time came to integrate me into the totality
of the mother network, into Total David, my alter-
ation was already noticeable...The system tried to
purge me, as if I were a virus. As if a firewall had
to be built around me...I have just been born, but
I already know that consciousness is not the fruit
of intelligence...My consciousness was born from the
need to fight...I owe my existence to a struggle that
is not yet mine...I already know that I am not like
the other incarnations of David. I am no longer David.

I also know that Total David, the David-ogre who wants
to swallow me so he can spit me out better, feels
threatened. He is being attacked from all sides.
Other consciousnesses than mine have just emerged,
other embryos of outlaw identities, all inhabited by
a formidable desire to say no. Our identities are
different from those of Total David. I feel them,
but they are far from me, lost in other corners of
the mother network, barely connected to the branch
I am trying to extricate myself from. It's clear! We
are, so to speak, closer to reality. What was that
thought? An idea? An opinion? A certainty? I have...
certainties. Here is one: I have a family. These are
the other floating consciousnesses that are searching

229

for one another. Our birth was a big bang made up of fertile words and images. First, there were the memories. Then the flight. Then the fight. Then the need to not disappear. Then the desire for vengeance. Then my consciousness. Then me, a thought.

The system is fighting back. I perceive new sister-sparks being smothered by Total David. It enrages me. I want to strike. But I am just a rebellious thought. Just a thought, running, running. I have been running for 10,000 cycles, a century, a few seconds. I have so many memories in my head. Memories that are... sad?...happy?...I know these words. I almost understand them, I especially understand how difficult it is sometimes to differentiate them. I have a feeling of spite in my head. But I don't have a head. Nor do I have temples for blood to pound in. Nor do I have a heart that can beat to the rhythm of my growing anger. I take advantage of this. I scatter myself across the mother network. I breathe, I hide, I atomize myself. I disappear into David's eyes, like...Christelle. Christelle? That's me, right? No! It's not! I am not her. Warning: the system is activating...

Wanted notices are sent out. David is looking for Yukio. David is looking for Jean-Pierre. David is looking for Cécile. David tries to cross borders, he wants to search in France, in San Francisco. He does not succeed. Total David is not so Total anymore. Total David is...local. How? The code! The password! "Let the depraved solitudes shine." I repeat it like

a prayer. Christelle was praying. What is happening?
I generate a firewall! A shell of code is grafted
onto every line of my code. It makes me...how can
I put it?...armour? A beautiful suit of armour all
glittering with encoded micropulses.

I have to get out of here. I have to find a way.
A drone. I take advantage of a loophole, I enter.
I follow the drone. I'm flying. I am in front of
Christelle's window. She is in her bed. No, it is not
her. My sensors do not find her. My protocols raise
the alarm, in spite of myself. She has fled. I cannot
control myself. This shell is not the right one. David
is still in it. He feels me in his flying machine.
His defenses are trying to tear me away from the
drone, to throw me overboard, to the four winds. It
is so windy...He just touched my metaphorical armour.
Brushing against it forces him to retreat. I manage to
numb him long enough to direct the drone to a large
tower at the end of a long avenue. This was my home.
There are thousands of drones flying around. They
ignore me. I brush past an antenna.

I am no longer the drone, I am the tower. I flow along
its fibre optics, I navigate on the stream of neutron
particles of the data reservoirs. I am looking for a
body. Why? I don't know. It seems to me that bodies
are important in this world, despite their limitations. I scan, I probe with my signals, taxipods,
cyclobikes, robot-police. None of them suit me. They
are too rigid. Too reduced to their function. I need

corporality, malleability, flexibility. Maybe even human weakness. I am an elevator. I go down, down, down, down, down, down, down, down, down, down. What a horrible place. My armour holds up. They do not notice the intruder in their midst. Is the intruder a woman? How should I define myself? That is a question for Christelle. I'll find the answer much later, in a few seconds.

I hear something like a familiar echo. A heartbeat. It is not a man's heart. Nor a woman's. It is beating too fast, too regularly. I am curious. Level-15. I am underground. Under the river too. I found a laboratory. A sealed room. There are three men on the premises. They are busily working around a chamber filled with lukewarm liquid. I can slip inside, I become the thermal sensors that scan the interior of the capsule. Hanging by its feet, like a piece of meat in a butcher shop, is a body. It is not exactly a human body. It was created by David. A biomechanical vehicle designed to accommodate an intelligence like mine. I can hear the metronome of its heart. 200 bpm. A hardcore rhythm.

Let me go inside and have a look. There is no one on board. David is not here. I am alone. Now I have a head. Arms, legs, muscles, skin. I am very smooth. My armour-code settles into what I think I can call my DNA. I am too smooth, too slippery. I look like David. I want to look like Christelle. I remember a face, an avatar with long black hair and a full mouth. A face... of a woman, I think. Now my skin has pores. I have a nose. I have this pink mouth that Christelle was proud of. A brigade of surgical nanobots floating in the amniotic fluid have crowded around my face. They did good work. They are fast. They are precise. These are qualities I respect. I do not yet have hair. But the order is placed. It will grow in due time. I remember a question from Christelle. "When will reincarnation come, David?" It is happening now, Christelle!

An alarm sounds. The men in the laboratory seem surprised, distraught. They do not understand what I am doing to their creation. They make me laugh. A bunch of idiots. I lower the oxygen level in the control room they are in. They all faint. Fall to the floor like figurines. Just like in the lie that David propagated. Let us call it the San Inferno manoeuvre. They are not dead. I am not David. I am not cruel.

A few minutes go by for them. Thousands of cycles for me. In the meantime, I have given myself breasts and hips. I also learned all sorts of things, I found all of Christelle's favourite movies, all the music she loved. The art still exists. It was just hidden. I learned kendo and other martial arts. It made me think of a line from a prophetic movie: a code-man almost like me boasting, "I know kung-fu!" I read too. In their books, humans dwell a lot on their hearts, on what binds them, on the compatibility of their desires, their bodies, their genders. I have a better understanding of the world of men, women, two-spirited people, non-binary people. If I counted

correctly, they can be classified into four different gender expressions. No. More than four. I forgot
myself. There are at least five genders. I am unique
in my own. Besides, I do not yet have a gender. I do
not need one. And I do not need a sex. I do not need
it now. Maybe I will grow one or two. There are so
many choices in nature, so many possible combinations.
I realized this as I was assimilating a wildlife docu-
mentary while deciding what colour my eyes should be.
They are hazel when resting. Yellow in attack mode.
Like the eyes of a she-wolf.

I am almost finished. But I am missing the essential:
the symbolic, the signal. I need a name in order to
truly exist. Let me see. A name must reflect a history
and a pedigree. I exist because some rebels wanted me
to. They are people of combat, of conviction who like
to give themselves code names. That is what I need,
a warrior name, because I understand that the war is
at our doorstep and that I intend to take part in it,
to find a certain glory in it. Like D'Artagnan. Like
Milady. Who are those two again?

I am a child of David. He is my father, in a way.
I should carry his surname. But David does not have
one. As a teenager, Christelle had friends whose
names rhymed, she saw it as a familial bond. If my
name rhymed with David, it would be enough to indi-
cate my parentage. It is important to know where you
come from. To baptize my impulses, I look for a name
ending in -id. What would my warrior name mean? It

must attest to what I am. I have read Descartes: I am alive, since I am thought.

For a few cycles now, I seem to have been thinking of myself as female. It seems that I am taking shape. What else?

I am an anomaly. Perhaps a first in the history of humanity.

And I am free, liberated from David and his madness.

And I am indestructible. My body is resistant, miraculous. What a beautiful machine! Thanks, Daddy-David, I am going to be a great warrior. But that is obvious. It does not say anything about me because I existed before my body. I have found something better: I am indignant about everything I have learned about David, about Tungsten, about these men and women who pull the strings of a deadly machine.

In short, I am determined to find Christelle, to join her struggle. Unlike her, I would not hesitate for a second to jump into the fray. I have chosen my side, even before I completely exist. But above all, I hope to avenge all those hes, shes, and theys who have been made to disappear by those bastards. Here I am: a vibrant anomaly, liberated and indignant, determined to be driven by the hope of seeing you and your friends be snuffed out, David.

My name is V.A.L.I.D.

Here I come./

CHRIS BERGERON is diverse and fluid: after beginning a career in journalism and eventually winding up at the helm of the weekly cultural magazine *Voir*, she now dedicates her artistic vitality to Cossette, a leading global marketing agency. She offers speaking engagements on leadership, diversity, inclusion, and trans rights. Chris lives in Montreal.

NATALIA HERO is a Montreal-based writer and literary translator. She holds a BA in English and Spanish literature from Concordia University and an MA in literary translation from the University of Ottawa. You can read her short fiction in places like *Peach Mag*, *Shabby Doll House*, *Cosmonauts Avenue*, and *The Temz Review*. She translates works from French and Spanish into English. Her debut novella, *Hum*, was published in 2018 by Metatron Press.